Sin shook his head. "Hardly. I'm taking my woman and my child to a safe, warm place."

"I'm not your woman, Sinclair," Bobbi said firmly. "Now, let me out of this car. Look, one night of..." She groped for the right words. She still didn't know how to describe what happened between them.

"I remember exactly what it was. And it was—"

"I don't need a description of our one night together," she said. "The important thing is that it's over. Please take the next exit and let me off." When he made no move, Bobbi sighed.

"The moment we reach a phone," she threatened, "I'll have you arrested. I'll take you to court."

"Bobbi, you're not the only one who made our baby. I did have something to do with it. So sit back and relax." Sin smiled wickedly. "Because I'm going to be around for a long, long time."

ABOUT THE AUTHOR

Muriel Jensen started writing in the sixth grade... and just never stopped. Marrying a journalist taught Muriel the art of discipline and the playful art of arguing whether it's easier to get the "who, what, when, where and why" in the first paragraph or to take 70,000 words in which to do it. Muriel lives in Astoria, Oregon, with her husband, two calico cats and a malamute named Deadline. She also has three grown children.

Books by Muriel Jensen

HARLEQUIN AMERICAN ROMANCE

Don't miss any of our special offers. Write to us at the following address for information on our newest releases.

Harlequin Reader Service
P.O. Box 1397, Buffalo, NY 14240
Canadian address: P.O. Box 603,
Fort Erie, Ont. L2A 5X3

MURIEL JENSEN

ONE AND ONE MAKES THREE

Harlequin Books

TORONTO • NEW YORK • LONDON
AMSTERDAM • PARIS • SYDNEY • HAMBURG
STOCKHOLM • ATHENS • TOKYO • MILAN
MADRID • WARSAW • BUDAPEST • AUCKLAND

Published March 1993

ISBN 0-373-16478-5

ONE AND ONE MAKES THREE

Prologue

April

Bobbi Perducci awoke with a start to the elegant resonance of church bells. The melody played against her consciousness—a little too loud but harmonious and somehow comforting. She settled back into the pillow without opening her eyes and smiled to herself, letting the long-forgotten warmth of a quiet Sunday morning ripple over her.

Then it occurred to her there were no churches in her neighborhood. She'd lived in Burbank for three years and never been awakened by church bells. The blissful dream state between sleep and wakefulness fell away and she opened her eyes in mild alarm.

Her eyes scanned a ceiling of light wood paneling and settled on a modern chandelier dripping long crystals. Sunlight touched it, making it look as though it were lit.

Her heart gave an unsettling little thud. Her bedroom ceiling was conventional southern California white blown-on texture with a half-bowl light fixture.

Then more inconsistencies flooded her awakening senses. She heard the roll of a gentle surf—a sound seldom available in inland Burbank. She saw unfamiliar curtains in a subtle moss and buff plaid drawn back against a blindingly blue sky. Where was the tree-shaded suburban street with its weekend sounds—laughing children, barking dogs, growling lawn mowers?

Now truly concerned, she lifted her head an inch off the pillow and looked down at a coverlet that matched the curtains. It was pulled up, quilted and plump, just under her breasts. And that was when she noticed the hand.

She heard her own little strangled gasp as though from a distance. A man's beautifully manicured, long-fingered hand cradled her right breast in its palm, the thumb resting on her nipple. She watched the pink bud bead as a wave of gooseflesh broke along her body— her clearly *naked* body.

With another whispered gasp she let her head fall back to the pillow and closed her eyes against the evidence of yet another of the now infamous Perils of Perducci.

God, she prayed silently, *let this be a hallucination.* Her fuzzy brain remembered a tall bottle of champagne, a balmy night, sand squishing between her toes and a lacy surf lapping at her ankles.

She remembered an arm around her shoulders, a comforting, rumbling voice in her ear, lips...warm, pliant, clever lips. But to whom had they belonged?

Oh, God. Her prayer took on an edge of desperation. This was no hallucination. *I've been celibate since Joey left. Whatever I've done—or whoever I did it with—it wasn't deliberate. I mean, if it had been, I'd remember, wouldn't I?* She winced at the wanton nature of her plea. *Forget the excuses, Lord. If I've been truly stupid, take me now.*

She waited prayerfully for the trumpet call of angels. It didn't come. Even the church bells stopped. All she heard now was the persistent roll of the surf and the sound of quiet breathing in her ear.

All right. She'd been stupid, but she'd never been a coward. What she had to do now was assess and control the damage.

The first step in that direction was learning the identity of the man who owned the hand that held her breast. Swallowing on a dry throat, she rolled her head to the left.

She saw crisp, golden hair. It was thick and rumpled and smelled of an herbal shampoo. It was the same rich color gaslight brought to a darkened room.

A wavy lock of it fell onto a broad forehead. His eyebrows were a slightly darker gold than his hair and one was quirked expressively, even in sleep.

And that was when it all came flooding back to her. She didn't have to see the bright blue eyes under the closed eyelids that were just beginning to stir, the strong, straight nose, the handsomely dimpled chin to remember.

This was Sin—in more ways that one. Yesterday, Paul Sinclair, attorney of note, bon vivant, and heir to a fortune, had been best man to her maid of honor when *her* best friend, Gina Raleigh, married *his* best friend, Patrick Gallagher.

She'd intended to go home right after the wedding. An interior designer was coming by to pick up two eighteenth-century mahogany corner chairs she was reupholstering. She hadn't intended to feel the great hole open in her life when Patrick and Gina drove off to the Candle Bay Inn Patrick owned on the Oregon Coast. She hadn't intended that a handsome, funny man she'd met only hours before would read her feelings and offer to take her for a walk on the beach. She hadn't intended for the walk to stretch into dinner, for him to have a wonderful house on the beach, a wonderful understanding of her need for laughter and friendship, a wonderful smile, a wonderful touch....

That was what got her into trouble every time, she thought, exasperated with herself. Orphaned in her teens, she'd learned to be strong and financially independent. She'd never be rich, but she'd never starve. She was intelligent and talented and disciplined.

But she was always trying to recapture what she'd lost when her parents died. She was always trying to rebuild that sense of family.

What a mess, she told herself as she gently and very slowly unclasped the male fingers that held her breast. Holding Sin's arm above her, Bobbi slipped sideways, inch by careful inch. Sin made an unintelligible sound, frowned and scooped her back toward him without opening his eyes.

She was now on her side, body to body with him, his warmth and the smells of his cologne and his maleness enclosing her, touching that needy little part of her that wanted a place in a man's arms, and tempted her to stay.

Then she remembered Joey Perducci, and the single woman's credo—"No man is better than the wrong man." Sinclair would definitely be the wrong man.

Slowly, deliberately, she began the tedious escape process again. This time she made it. She found her panties beside the bed, her hose on the carpet at the foot of it. One of the bedposts wore one cup of her bra like a hat. With a horrified little groan she snatched it and put it on as she searched for her sweater and pants. She found them together beyond the door, a jumble of red and black on the bone-colored carpet of the gallery that looked down onto the vaulted-ceilinged living room. A part of her mind not concerned with getting her out of there was taken aback by the expensive chic of her surroundings.

Shoes. Where were her shoes? She found one hanging from the pointed ear of an African mask over the fireplace. She began an immediate search for the second one, refusing to consider how the first one had gotten there. She was about to leave without it, sure her host would awaken at any moment, when she spotted it inside a trophy case in an oak and leather study. Its heel protruded from a very large cup inscribed with the year 1988 and the words City of Angels Regatta.

Hopping on one foot as she put on the shoe, she headed for the door, temper beginning to rise.

Certainly she'd been stupid, but *he* was hardly blameless. He'd gotten her drunk, played on her need for companionship and conversation and parlayed it into a night to remember.

No, that wasn't fair. The details of the night before were definitely fuzzy, but she was sure she'd remember anything unpleasant. He hadn't dragged her on the moonlit walk along the beach, he hadn't poured the champagne down her throat and he hadn't made her susceptible to his charm and his romantic attentions. She'd been vulnerable, and that was her own fault.

She reached for the doorknob, considering herself lucky to have almost made her escape without waking him when she remembered her purse. She hadn't seen it when she'd searched for her shoes, she realized unhappily. It had to be upstairs. She couldn't get a cab without it.

He was still asleep on his side when she tiptoed into the room. His arm was flung out as though it still held her. Moving cautiously, she scanned the room, then checked under the bed. Nothing.

She was close to panic, thinking about car keys, driver's license, credit cards, makeup, when she noticed the yawning cavity of the bathroom door.

It could hardly be called simply a bathroom, she thought as she stopped on the threshold in wonder. It had a sunken tub, a separate shower, a dressing area, a deep window seat filled with plants, and the other side of the fireplace that was also in the bedroom. She checked every surface and every cupboard, resigned to having to report her cards and her license lost, when she found her small saddlebag purse hanging by its shoulder strap from the shower head. What *had* they done last night?

She snatched it down and hurried out into the bedroom—to be stopped dead by the sight of Sin sitting up against the pillows. He looked broad and sexy and, despite all she'd told herself in the past few minutes, very tempting.

That expressive eyebrow rose and he smiled. "I thought we'd have breakfast in bed," he said in that quiet, rumbly voice.

For a moment it was as though something tied her to him and she felt a tangible tug in his direction. Then she suddenly saw the big picture—the gorgeous blond playboy in his bachelor surroundings, and she, Bobbi Perducci, in her small garage workshop that reeked of glue and stain and varnish. It would never work. He was the wrong man.

She pulled herself up to her sturdy five foot eight and blew him a kiss as she walked to the bedroom door. "You'd better order out, Sin. Good luck with... everything."

She closed the door behind her and leaned against it with a wince. *Good luck with everything?* Brilliant exit line. His confused expression as she walked out the door told her he had no idea what she'd meant, either.

What did one say to a man with whom one had just been intimate on eight hours' acquaintance and would never see again? She followed the only course she could think of. She ran.

PAUL SINCLAIR leaned back in his desk chair and stared moodily at Bobbi Perducci's red cloisonné earrings. He'd noticed them that unforgettable evening a week ago today because they'd been the same shade as her sweater.

During Patrick and Gina's wedding, Bobbi had been a cool column of gray silk behind the bride. But afterward, when they'd all changed clothes and gone to lunch before the Gallaghers left for Oregon, she'd appeared in slim black pants, a soft red sweater and a smile that had lowered all his defenses.

At the moment, the earrings hung in a diagonal row on the corkboard cube on his desk that held pens and pencils and his scrimshaw handled letter opener. He'd put the backs into the velvet box in the wall safe that held the tie clips and cuff links he kept at the office for those social occasions when there wasn't time to go home and change.

She'd left them at his place the morning she'd walked out of his room as though she'd just demonstrated Tupperware or given a crystal party. It still made him steam to think about it.

The most infuriating part was, he didn't know how to explain her behavior. And he didn't like things or people he didn't understand.

The night before, she'd been charming and sweet, and touchingly vulnerable in a way he hadn't seen in a woman since high school. He'd had his share of amorous nights but he hadn't had an evening that had been so...significant in a long time.

He'd just about convinced himself he'd found a new breed of woman—then she'd awakened, acted as though it had all been just another encounter and left.

He traced one cloisonné heart with his long index finger. She'd burst his bubble all right. He pushed aside the stack of case files on his desk and gave the corkboard cube a spin. He stopped it when he found the telephone number he'd looked up days ago and pinned to it, certain she would call first. Women always called him back.

He reached for the phone, dialed the number, then changed his mind before the second ring and cradled the receiver. No. She'd call.

He smiled in satisfaction as the phone warbled its electronic ring.

"Paul Sinclair," he said quietly.

"Sin. It's Patrick."

A pang of disappointment slapped him down, but he quickly put it aside.

"Hey!" The sound of his friend's voice, friendly and uncomplicated, after his own confusing week of daydreaming about a woman made sanity return. "Got to Candle Bay safe and sound?"

"In a manner of speaking," Patrick returned dryly.

Sin frowned into the phone. "What do you mean? What happened?"

"It's a long story. Look, I'm sending you a check, and I need you to do a few things for me."

The few things involved sending money to a motel owner they'd run out on before paying their bill in Santa Cruz, an automobile dealer from whom they'd "borrowed" a car in Rockport, and with whom they'd left Patrick's truck.

"You left your truck there?" Sin demanded in disbelief. "What are you driving?"

"A Volkswagen bus."

"What? Tell me you're kidding."

"Like I said, it's a long story. Will you do it?"

"You two have a Bonnie and Clyde honeymoon?"

"Sin . . ."

"Of course I'll do it."

"Thanks. You still planning to come up and spend Memorial Day weekend with us?"

Had Bobbi called, Sin might have made other plans. As it was . . . "Sure."

"Good. Can you pick up Bobbi and bring her along? I know Gina'd love to see her. She's had a pretty tough week."

"Is she all right?" Sin asked in confusion and concern.

"She's great."

Patrick reminded Sin of what he'd like him to do, and Sin assured him that he would. They exchanged a few insults and a few pleasantries, then Patrick hung up.

Sin replaced the receiver, trying to piece together a scenario for his friends' honeymoon, using the facts he'd just learned. All he could conclude was that they'd run out on a hotel bill and stolen a Volkswagen bus.

He stared consideringly at the earrings. He'd get the details filled in over the holiday weekend. The important facts now were that his friends were fine, and he had a legitimate reason to call Bobbi. But there were still four weeks until Memorial Day. He'd give it a couple of weeks so she didn't think the call had anything to do with the other night.

When he made love to her in Candle Bay, he'd return the earrings.

Chapter One

Bobbi pulled up in front of the Georgian mansion set back on a high, grassy bank. The house was aglow with lights that gleamed off the long line of costly sports cars lining the circular driveway of the exclusive Beverly Hills address.

Though her hostess, Rebecca Fox, had insisted she come, Bobbi felt sure her absence wouldn't be noticed in this collection of upper class people gathered to celebrate the host's birthday. Bobbi had refinished the Georgian walnut pedestal desk that was Mrs. Fox's present to her husband. The woman's pleasure at the excellence of Bobbi's work had prompted the invitation.

And that had been that.

Bobbi started up the driveway with trepidation, her high heels clicking loudly on the pavement. She smoothed the front of the simple black trapeze dress she'd bought for the occasion. She checked the French cuffs just above her elbow with their pearl buttons that matched the buttons down the front. She stopped at the door, giving everything one final tug into place.

Then the door opened on her without warning and a smiling butler bowed her into a wide foyer. Parquet flooring gleamed, a crystal chandelier shone and Bobbi had to withhold a gasp at the opulence of the beautiful home's interior.

Beyond the foyer crowds of people moved through large rooms on either side. She caught a glimpse of antiques and artwork and a plush white carpet that was absolutely pristine.

She dealt with people of the Foxes' social standing on a fairly regular basis now, but always in her workshop, never in their homes. And usually one at a time, not in large groups. She felt uncomfortable and sorely out of place.

Her hostess, Rebecca, came toward her in a pale blue dress that clung lovingly to a high bosom and taut hips. "Bobbi!" Rebecca wrapped her in an embrace. "I thought you'd find some excuse to back out on me."

"I didn't dare," Bobbi replied. "But I really can't stay very..."

"Nonsense." Rebecca hooked an arm in hers and led her toward the crowd of people to the right of the foyer. "I know what's going on in your mind, but these are just people. A little loud, a little showy, but all good friends. You'll like them once you get to know them."

She wanted to say there was little point in getting to know them; she'd never see them again. But that sounded so sarcastic she kept it to herself.

"I know just the person," Rebecca went on, "to help you get acquainted and feel more comfortable."

They seemed to be heading toward a knot of people in conversation. A middle-aged woman too plump for her long silver lamé jacket turned away from the little group as Rebecca and Bobbi approached. Bobbi gave her a tentative smile, thinking that despite her outfit, the woman looked motherly. She would stay half an hour, then she would plead a headache and make her escape.

"Claudia," Rebecca said to the woman, "your David's in the library with Ridley and Dennis Weston. They're probably playing poker. Will you see if you can break it up? It's almost time for cake and presents. This is Bobbi Perducci, by the way."

Claudia's eyes widened with respect. "You did a wonderful job. Becky gave me a sneak preview this afternoon. Ridley will be thrilled. I know this isn't the place to bring it up, but I have an antique wicker rocker I've tried to repair myself and botched. Do you think you could save it?"

"I'd be happy to try," Bobbi said. "Rebecca can give you the address of my shop."

"Wonderful!" Looking pleased, Claudia went off to break up the poker game.

Bobbi watched her go in alarm. So that comfortable looking woman hadn't been her intended protectress?

"Sin, darling."

Bobbi's head snapped around at the sound of the name just in time to see Rebecca reach her free hand into the dark suit-coated arm of a man whose back was turned to them.

Bobbi recognized the hand that held a tulip glass of champagne before its owner turned completely in their direction.

No, she thought. *It can't be.* After Memorial Day weekend in Candle Bay, she'd hoped never to see him again. Who'd have suspected he'd turn up here, at the home of a client?

Then she looked up into a pair of blue eyes that had lived in her memory for four months, and felt herself go a little weak in the knees.

Paul Sinclair's gold hair had been slicked back for this semiformal occasion, and even now near his hairline, curls fought the restriction. That expressive eyebrow went up and a lazy smile showed strong white teeth.

"Sin, this is Bobbi Perducci," Rebecca said, freeing Bobbi's arm so that she had little recourse but to offer to shake Sin's extended hand. "She restored Ridley's desk."

"Ah." He nodded as he shook her hand, a sparkle of amusement in his eyes as he apparently waited to see if she would admit to their having already been acquainted.

Honesty was usually the best policy, she thought, but at the moment, it didn't seem wise.

"Mr. Sinclair." She forced an interested smile. Her mind was coping with the far-reaching effects of her unbelievable bad luck, while trying to concoct a plan that would allow her immediate retreat.

"Miss Perducci." He inclined his head and kept her hand as he reached behind him to place his glass on a coaster on the grand piano. He *was* playing the game.

"Mrs." she corrected.

That expressive eyebrow raised higher in pretended surprise. "Widowed?"

This duplicity was already beginning to deepen her discomfort. "Divorced."

"Becky showed me the desk last night," he said, the sparkle in his eyes igniting as he added with all innocence. "You do excellent work."

The implication that he was referring to something other than her skill as a furniture restorer was not lost on Bobbi. She fought desperately to hold the rush of color back and looked him straight in the eye.

"It's simply a matter of getting things down to the bare material," she said.

She had the satisfaction of seeing surprise in his eyes. She was a little surprised herself.

"I suppose," he said, "that you have considerable experience."

She nodded modestly. "That's how I avoid being taken in by rip-offs."

Rebecca frowned from one to the other then gave Sin's arm a light shake. "Darling, you promised to take Bobbi under your wing tonight. And I don't want you to talk about her work. She's already gotten a job from Claudia Buckley and she'd only been in the house five minutes. She works like a little slave in that shop. She needs a break. I want her to have fun tonight."

He sent another innocent glance in Bobbi's direction. "I'll see to it, Becky," he said gravely.

Then Becky was off, leaving them somehow alone in a room crowded with people.

Sin looked down at Bobbi and couldn't figure out what the hell it was about her that continued to haunt him. Her cat-green eyes were pretty, though studying him suspiciously at the moment. Her mouth was wide and smirking at him rather than smiling. She did have hair the color of the moon, but wore it in a jagged, irregular cut. In her black dress, she looked very much like a smug tuxedo cat.

He'd tried not to think of her since that interminable weekend in Candle Bay. He had hoped to recapture the delicious mood of that night after their friends' wedding, but she'd been a shrew the entire weekend, from the moment he'd picked her up for the drive to LAX, until he'd dropped her off at her place after the flight back.

He still had her earrings.

But he could still see the curves of her body in his mind's eye, and nothing had shaken his impressions of that night after the wedding. He saw her under him, against the bank of pillows on his bed. Her eyes had been soft then, not suspicious. And her smile had been sweet and real. If he closed his eyes now, he knew he could conjure immediately the feel of her nipples against his ribs.

To his consternation, he felt it happen even now in a crowded room with his eyes open.

"You *knew* I would be here tonight," she said quietly, her tone accusing.

He reached for his champagne and took a sip. "Yes," he admitted. He'd decided it was time to deal with her once and for all.

"And yet you came anyway."

The eyebrow came down in a frown of confusion. "Of course. I was invited. I've been the Foxes' lawyer since I joined my father's firm." He knew she was baiting him. He was willing to be baited. "Why? Should I have stayed away to save you embarrassment?"

She was jogged against him as a waiter came through with a tray of glasses. Sin held her to him with a hand splayed against her back. He put his glass down and reached for another from the tray. He released her the moment the waiter moved on, then offered her the glass.

Every part of her that had touched him was shuddering. She pushed the proffered glass back toward him, exerting mind over matter to stop her hand from trembling.

"No, thank you," she said coolly.

He studied her a moment in confusion. "I seem to remember that you're particularly fond of champagne," he said softly.

She glared at him for his continued suggestions of intimate knowledge. "I've changed my ways."

"It'll relax you."

"I'm relaxed."

"You're shaking."

She drew an exasperated breath and took the glass from him with a yank. Both of them stepped back as champagne sloshed onto the carpet.

She groaned guiltily.

"White on white," Sin said, hooking the piano bench with his shoe and pulling it to cover the minute spot. "No one will notice."

She handed him his glass and put hers in its place on the coaster. She leaned her elbow on the piano.

"To answer your previous question," she said, striving for a calmer, quieter demeanor, "I thought you'd stay away once you knew I was coming, to save *yourself* embarrassment."

He returned a greeting from a couple passing through the press of people, then focused his lazy blue eyes on Bobbi. "Should I be embarrassed?"

She considered him, anger trying to ruffle her new calm. She refused to let it. "I'm not sure. I'm unfamiliar with how your social strata conducts itself."

A flare of temper showed under the laziness. "I'm not aware of stratae," he said quietly. "I work with all kinds of people. If you're conscious of social strata, you're the one who should be embarrassed."

She was, and that made her angry. "You know what I mean," she whispered, grateful that the party's noise level isolated them and their argument.

He sipped from the glass. "Why don't you explain it to me?"

"All right." She swiped a hand at the spiky wisps of hair on her forehead. Sin got a sharp mental image of having done that himself in the middle of that night four months ago. He made himself concentrate on what she was saying. "You're a cad."

He stared at her a moment, then finally smiled, unable to hold it back. "That sounds like something Claudette Colbert would have said to Clark Gable in the thirties."

"All right," she said. Subtlety wasn't working. Her voice was rising. She looked around, saw that no one had noticed, and lowered it deliberately. "You could have called."

"I did," he replied. "We flew to Candle Bay together, remember?"

"Patrick made you make that call. But you hadn't called before, and you haven't called since."

He did not look embarrassed or even remotely guilty. He took another sip of champagne. "Why should I have?"

Bobbi let the question hang there in silence. Had she been alone with him, and had no one to consider but herself, she'd have doubled her fist and belted him right in the chops. In fact, it would be so satisfying, that she gave the notion a second thought.

Sin read the violence in her eyes and decided it was time to take their discussion to the garden.

"Come on." He put his glass on a waiter's tray and caught Bobbi's hand, pulling her with him to the French doors that led to the patio. They'd just cleared the patio steps and started down a walk protected from view by high, fragrant hedges when she yanked away from him and reared back.

He caught her fist in one rock-steady palm and held it there, inches from his face, his fingertips biting into her slender bones.

"I didn't call," he said, his casual facade now replaced by judicious anger, "because *you* walked out on me with a wave and a 'Good luck with everything.'"

She yanked her fist from his grip. "Well, pardon me for wishing you well!"

"I thought that implied," he said slowly and clearly, as though to someone unfamiliar with the language, "that you were putting an end to it before it really started. That you had another relationship and that night had just been another..."

"*Before* it started?" she repeated loudly. "You don't consider going to bed together as starting a relationship?"

He admonished just as loudly, "You're doing it again. You're blaming me for what you did. I was willing to start something." He jabbed an index finger into her shoulder. "You're the one who walked out with an oh-so-casual 'Thanks for the toss in the sheets, Sinclair. See you around.'"

Bobbi blinked up at him, caught off guard by his vehemence. Confused by an attitude she hadn't expected, she focused on the only thing she was sure about. "I never said that."

"I was paraphrasing. That was clearly the impression you left." He caught her elbow, guiding her along with him as he headed for a well-lit pond in the middle of acres of lawn.

She flexed her hand to restore blood flow, trying desperately to recall how she'd felt at the moment he described. "I knew it could never be anything," she said finally.

"Why not?"

She looked up at him impatiently. "You're rich."

He made a scornful sound. "So, sue me. I inherited."

"So, it scared me."

"Why?"

They'd cleared the hedge and he guided her toward the stone bench near the pond. Small splashes and ripples disturbed the smooth surface, crickets chirped and somewhere in the distance was the lonely sound of a night bird.

He leaned down to run a hand over the bench. "Clean and dry," he said, gesturing Bobbi to sit. "Becky always sees to every detail. Why does my having money scare you?"

She probed her mind for words that would make it sound logical—mostly, because it wasn't. "My marriage was mercifully short and taught me a few lessons I'll never forget. Number one was, never get involved with a playboy."

His eyebrow went up. It amazed her how many different emotions it could express. At the moment, it seemed to indicate confusion.

"You told me at the wedding lunch that he traveled from city to city with a bungy-jumping bucket on a crane. There aren't many in my *social strata* . . ." He repeated her words with exaggerated precision, "who do that. I fail to see the connection."

"He hadn't a care in the world," she explained. "He did what he wanted to do without consideration for how anyone else would be affected. I worked long hours to get the bills paid while he spent his time taking the bucket to carnivals and county fairs. He usually came home without any money." She gave a prideful toss of her head. "He found other ways to spend it."

Sin was less offended than mystified. "And I remind you of him?"

"You're free to come and go as you please," she said. "If you get bored with life, you can just walk away. Wealth allows you that option. I'm looking for a man with staying power."

He frowned, trying to sift through her argument. "You're saying if I *didn't* have money, I'd have staying power, yet your husband wasn't wealthy, but he still left. That doesn't come together, Bobbi."

"It's an attitude," Bobbi insisted. Her green gaze met his blue one. "Tell me that you haven't entertained a long string of women in that beautiful bedroom."

"I prefer them one at a time."

"You know what I mean," she scolded quietly.

He nodded. "I do, and it's ridiculous. You can't judge one man by another, even if they have similarities in common which I assure you would be hard to find in the case of a guy involved with door-to-door bungy jumping and myself. But apart from that, there's another important point you're overlooking.''

"Oh?"

He loved the imperious tilt of her chin when she said that. He couldn't wait to dimple it with a few well-chosen words.

"If you ran out on me that morning because you were so sure nothing could develop between us..."

He paused and she waited out the silence, her eyes wide and interested.

"Why," he asked, "are you upset that I didn't call?"

She bluffed it out for ten seconds. Dignity wouldn't allow her to admit he had a point.

He leaned an elbow between them on the back of the bench and said, "I'll tell you why. Because despite all your unreasonable reasons to the contrary, you'd like something to develop between us."

She closed her eyes and made a sound of exasperation. "Please," she said dryly and tried to push herself to her feet. But he held her shoulder to the bench with a firm hand.

"It's all right," he assured her. "I understand. I feel the same way."

Her heart gave a hopeful little bump she prayed he hadn't felt against his fingertips. She looked up at him with a practiced casualness. "What do you mean?"

"We're physical dynamite," he said. "But we know we're incompatible in other ways. So, here we are, caught in a push and pull that generates a lot of energy. You turn yours into anger."

Her little leap of hope crashed. She was going to try again to hit him any minute now. "Pray tell, Freud," she asked, "what do you do with yours?"

"Store it. Turn it in a positive direction."

"And what would that be?"

"You really want to know?"

She knew. She'd have to be a fool not to know. Sexual electricity charged the air around them, raised gooseflesh on her arms and caused a tingling sensation along her spine.

A sense of self-preservation warred with vivid memories of what it was like to be held by him, what it was like when he kissed her. The memories would live with her; they'd both seen to that, but she found herself wanting to feel the reality of it one more time. Then she came to her senses.

She opened her mouth and turned to him to tell him in no uncertain terms what she thought of his arrogance. And that little gesture played right into his hands.

He pulled her into the curve of his shoulder and invaded her parted lips, recalling for her without preamble the intimacy they'd shared. Slowly, artfully, he probed the sweet depths of her mouth, his hands roving her back, the swell of her hip, the line of her thigh. She defeated herself by pulling him toward her rather than pushing him away.

In the dark she was sharply aware of his every touch. Her mouth, her jaw, her throat reacted to his lips. And deep inside her, the heart of her femininity fisted as though waiting, preparing. She heard herself gasp into his kiss.

Sin didn't understand why he felt this way. That night with her four months ago had stayed with him as if it were some kind of physical memory, even when the weekend in Candle Bay should have counterbalanced it.

And now it was reality again. He felt her immediate and lively response, her mobile, taunting fingers along his shoulders, up his neck, into his hair. The rub of her breasts against the front of his shirt made him long to tear the fabrics from between them. Her leg swept along his causing a shudder in him that threatened dire consequences.

He pulled her away to hold her at arm's length, looking for some kind of an explanation in her eyes. What the hell was this? She looked as surprised and confused as he felt.

Assuming an air of control, he said with feigned amusement, "Now, isn't that a sweeter use of energy than anger?" Actually he was beginning to think this wasn't amusing at all.

Bobbi didn't know what to say. She was sure her eyes reflected what she felt and would make a lie of any denial. But before she could respond, a feminine shout came from the patio.

"Sin? Bobbi!" It was Rebecca's voice.

"Here!" Bobbi called, relieved to have a diversion from Sin's knowing look. She turned hurriedly back to the house, Sin following slowly behind her.

Rebecca appeared faintly embarrassed. "I hope I didn't...I mean, I didn't mean to...well, Ridley's about to open his presents and I'm going to unveil the desk. I know he'll want to thank you, Bobbi."

"Sin was just showing me the pond," Bobbi said brightly.

Rebecca studied her pink cheeks and smiled, apparently pleased about something. "Good. Well, come on inside. We need every able voice to sing Happy Birthday."

The large room where gifts had been stacked was packed with guests. Ridley Fox, looking embarrassed, was already tearing into the first box. Behind him, against the wall, a long, low shape was covered with a tarpaulin on which flowers had been painted and a large bow attached. The desk. Men who'd found chairs for their ladies rimmed the room, blocking the view of the host.

"Oh, dear," Rebecca grumbled in concern. "I did want Bobbi to be able to see."

"I'll take care of that." Sin tugged Bobbi to the piano in the far corner of the room and bracketing her waist in his large hands, hoisted her onto it. She landed with a little squeal of surprise in a flutter of black crepe and black-stockinged legs.

Sin leaned an elbow beside her, his arm touching her thigh, and ignored her mild indignation as the ritual of gift-opening proceeded.

Rebecca's husband seemed like someone she'd like to know, Bobbi thought, watching him express pleasure and gratitude over his gifts. She imagined he would love the desk.

He did. While Rebecca played a flourish on the piano, winking at Bobbi, Ridley swept the tarpaulin off and stared. In the bright light, the veneer shone like a polished jewel, including a small square she'd patched on one corner and made nearly invisible.

He ran a reverent hand over it, looking up at Rebecca with clearly obvious delight. Everyone in the room crowded in for a closer look.

"This is the young lady responsible," Rebecca boasted, gesturing like a magician in Bobbi's direction.

"Oh, God," Bobbi groaned under her breath, seriously considering a leap off the piano.

"Stay there," Sin said softly, grinning up at her. "You should be exuding confidence, not cringing in embarrassment."

"Bobbi Perducci," Rebecca went on with her introduction. "She brings old treasures back to life in a little shop in Burbank."

There was a smattering of applause. Bobbi was immediately approached by an old woman with a lorgnette. Then Bobbi realized it wasn't a lorgnette at all, but a pair of eyeglasses with one of the lenses out. The woman wore a lacy dress in neon pink with matching lace-up shoes. Bobbi tried desperately to concentrate on the woman's face and not the outlandish footwear.

"Perducci." The woman studied Bobbi a moment then rapped Sin in the chest with a folded fan. "What's your connection with this girl, Sinclair?"

Sin smiled down at the woman. "Friend, Jessie. Bobbi, may I present Jessica Dulcich. Jessie, Bobbi Perducci."

"Nothing to do with the mafia, I hope."

"No," Bobbi replied simply, stifling a need to laugh when she realized the question had been seriously asked.

"Good. Like my money to get into good hands, not bad. And you never know about Italian names. Don't have it to waste, you know."

Bobbi thought she might have guessed that by the resourceful use of the woman's broken eyeglasses. But the dress, though truly frightful, appeared expensive. And she guessed the satin lace-ups had probably been specially made.

"And you do have good hands, girl. Think you can do anything with a sewing rocker? Drawer's completely out of it. No great value. Was my grandmother's."

Sin frowned. "A chair with a drawer in it?"

Bobbi nodded. "Under the seat. Really very convenient when you think about it. Ladies kept needlework supplies in it."

She gave Jessie her stock phrase. "I'll be happy to look at it. I'm no carpenter, but I work with one."

"Good." She wanged her on the knee with the fan. "I'll have my son bring it by." She looked up at Sin with a roll of her eyes and a shake of her head. "Friend," she said scornfully. "Thought you had a brain, Sinclair."

"First impressions *can* be deceiving," Bobbi said, straight-faced.

Sin looked up at her, that eyebrow raised to mark reluctant amusement.

"My first impression of *this* boy," Jessie said, tapping him with the fan again on the chance there was some doubt who she was talking about, "was when he was about four hours old. Knew then he'd be a problem. All the other babies were asleep and he had all the nurses running around, trying to quiet him down." She tapped him again, an indulgent smile revealing her true feelings. "When you going to have my will ready?"

"By your appointment on Tuesday," Sin replied, taking the fan from her and tucking it into his breast pocket. "I'll keep this so you don't get arrested. I wouldn't know how to explain to a judge that my client massacred all the guests at a party with a paper fan."

Laughing, she snatched it back from him, threatening him with it yet again.

"You hit me with that thing one more time, Jessie," he warned, "and I'll make you do a living will."

"I will *not*," she said imperiously, "appear before a camera so that all my relatives can laugh at me when I'm gone."

"Then you will *not*," he said, "hit me again, or as your attorney I will insist that you put your will on videotape."

She glared at him and when he didn't flinch, smiled. "What time Tuesday?"

"Two o'clock."

"I'll be there."

"See that you're on time."

"Smart-mouthed young puppy!"

"Beautiful sexpot."

Jessie walked away in a gale of laughter.

Bobbi watched her go and shook her head in amazement. "A woman who knows how to deal with you. I like that."

Sin smiled affectionately after Jessie. "Longtime friend of the family. Her husband and my grandfather were in business together until her husband died. Since then she's managed her investments like a genius and spent her free time poking into the lives of everyone she cares about."

"She's very straightforward."

"She insists that subtlety is confusing, and diplomacy slows things down. According to my mother she should be called Jessie the Juggernaut. Get out of her way or be prepared to be rolled over."

Bobbi looked down into his eyes from her high perch, intrigued suddenly by the idea that Sin hadn't sprung fully formed on some fashionable corner of Rodeo Drive. She had a vague memory of Gina telling her that he'd grown up lonely, too.

"Do your parents live in L.A.?" she asked.

"From time to time," he replied. His mood altered subtly to one of stiffness, but returned almost instantly to his patient good humor. "They do a lot of traveling. They're international lawyers. Along with a friend of theirs from law school, they started the firm to which I belong. Their partner handled the domestic stuff. When I got out of school, he was ready to retire, so I took over for him. My parents have a place in London, one in Hong Kong and a yacht in Sydney.''

''Wow,'' she said quietly, unable to withhold the sound of envy.

He studied her wide eyes. ''Foreign travel appeals to you?''

''In a way,'' she admitted. Then she smiled—a genuine smile—he noticed, not one of the phony ones she reserved for him. ''But I wouldn't want to go jetting everywhere. I'd love to take a walking tour of Europe. Examine every little country lane, every hill, every ruin, every sidewalk café and country market.''

Sin smiled back, unaware how sincere his own smile was. ''That's how I feel about sailing. I'd like to catch a honey wind and visit every little cove or harbor from Newport, Rhode Island, to Lahaina.''

Bobbi looked down at him, seeing the deep blue water of a summer sea in his eyes. For a moment she could feel herself on the deck of a boat, the sun on her face and the wind in her hair.

Sin straightened away from the piano, snared by the unfocused look in her eyes. He could see the spring green of the Hampshire countryside there and imagined himself walking beside her, backpacks on their shoulders, as they followed a lane that meandered forever over hill after hill.

''Cake.'' Ridley suddenly appeared before them, handing each of them a plate. He had loosened his tie and was beaming.

"Bobbi," he said with obvious heartfelt sincerity, "I can't tell you how much I appreciate the work that went into my desk. I've wanted one for years. I suppose Becky told you."

Bobbi nodded, feeling almost as pleased as he appeared. "She did. She was so excited to find it for you. I'm glad you're as happy with it as she thought you'd be."

He glanced over his shoulder to be sure no one was listening. "I've been on the lookout for a fainting couch for her. Do you think you can help?"

She nodded, eager to do so. Another party like this one, she thought wryly, and she'd be on easy street. "Of course. I'm always watching for special pieces."

He winked. "I'll be in touch from the office. She knows everything that goes on within a five-mile radius of this house."

"I'll keep my eyes open in the meantime."

Ridley turned his attention on Sin as though he'd just noticed him. "What do you hear from your folks?"

"Ah . . ." Bobbi saw his instant's hesitation, then he replied with all affability, "My secretary read in *W* just this morning that they were dining Upstairs at the Savoy. The Burton-Chambers merger must be going well."

Ridley clapped him on the shoulder. "Good. Good. Did Becky talk to you about the trust for our new granddaughter?"

"I'll have it ready for you on Friday."

"All right." He started to walk away, then turned back to tilt his head at Bobbi while fixing his teasing gaze on Sin. "I'd consider a little billable time in Bobbi's direction if I were you."

Sin glanced her way innocently. "Would you?"

Ridley leaned closer as though he shared an important secret. "She's very pretty, for one thing. And you'd be saved from ever having to give up your favorite chair because it was no longer presentable. She could just redo it for you. See you Friday."

Sin leaned against the piano beside Bobbi, forked a piece of cake into his mouth, chewed and swallowed. "He obviously doesn't know," he said, casting her a sideways glance, "how you feel about our 'social strata.'"

Bobbi poked at a ripple of frosting with the tine of her fork. "Could we forget I said that?" she asked. "It was a poor choice of words, and not precisely what I meant anyway."

He took another bite of cake, made a sound of disapproval, then looked for a safe surface on which to place the plate. He decided on the piano bench tucked under the keyboard.

"What *did* you mean?" he asked, now leaning an elbow on the piano so that he could look up into her face.

She sighed over his persistence and let her fork drop onto her plate. "That we come from two different worlds," she said, striving for patience. She had to keep reminding herself that, though he was responsible for not calling her, what happened that night wasn't solely his fault. She'd been an eager participant.

"Trite, but true," he said, "but this is the age of the shrinking planet. People once separated by opposing ideologies as well as actual walls are now coming together as friends."

It was dangerous to look into his eyes. She'd learned that four months ago and the intervening time didn't seem to have changed that. "You want to be friends?" she asked softly.

"Don't you?"

That might be the answer, she thought. Since a permanent relationship was out of the question—not that he'd even asked her—friendship would keep them in proximity. Trapped in his gaze, she let herself believe that could work. Then she realized she'd be courting disaster.

"No," she said firmly, putting her plate down beside her on the napkin. "I don't think that's workable, either."

Sin thought she was probably right. Still, something in her tone did not convince him. Deep in her eyes another message was visible—and yanked at him.

The strains of live mellow music began to drift out from the other side of the foyer where several couples were already dancing.

She looked suddenly edgy, even a little pale. "I have to go," she said. "I have two chairs to deliver first thing in the morning." She braced her hands on the piano, prepared to leap down.

He caught her waist and held her there.

"If this is goodbye," he said, feeling the flutter of her heart under his thumb. "I'd like a dance before you leave."

"Sin..."

He lifted her off the piano, holding her suspended for a moment, his eyes looking up into hers, her hands pushing ineffectively against his shoulders. She looked half annoyed and all aflutter.

"People are looking," she whispered, her eyes darting from the guests behind him, to his upturned face. "Put me down this minute."

"If you promise to dance with me."

"What will that prove?" she demanded under her breath.

"We both know we're throwing aside something that could have been important," he said. "The dance will give us something to remember."

That was an ironic choice of words, she thought with a wry little smile. She'd have very little trouble remembering him.

Behind him, people were pointing and smiling. Rebecca, who was halfway across the room with her arm in Ridley's, turned to see what everyone was looking at. She stopped, looking like an indulgent parent.

"All right!" Bobbi said to Sin. "Just put me down."

He did, then led her past the interested onlookers to the middle of the floor where other couples swayed to the moody music.

He took her lightly into his arms and she knew immediately this was going to be a mistake. It brought swiftly, clearly to mind the midnight dance they'd enjoyed in Sin's bed with the surf crashing beyond the window.

Instinctively she tried to pull away, but he pulled her back, holding her firmly against him. "Come on," he scolded quietly. "You promised."

She had. She should just allow herself to enjoy this moment with him. She wanted it as much as he did. She chided herself for being such a wimp and made a conscious effort to relax. She found it difficult with Sin's arms wrapped around her waist, his muscled thigh moving between hers.

"That's it." One big hand rubbed gently between her shoulder blades. "For a minute there you felt like a corset without a woman in it."

Sensation sped along her spine. She wriggled slightly to shake it off and succeeded only in stirring a tingle in her breasts as they rubbed against his jacket. She drew a deep breath of frustration—another mistake.

Sin took her arms and placed them around his neck. "I'm not going to bite," he assured her, then he grinned. "Although I do remember that you liked that."

She stopped moving and glared up at him. "Sinclair, if you don't—"

"All right, all right." He pulled her closer and fell into step with the music. "We'll talk about something harmless. We could talk about your business. I think you've really broadened your customer base tonight. If Jessie's pleased with your work, she'll tell everyone. Of course, she'll tell everyone if she *isn't* pleased."

"A scary thought," Bobbi said, trying to concentrate on stringing words together to avoid thinking about their bodies in contact. "Do you represent everyone in this room?"

He had dropped his cheek to lean it against hers and sighed softly against it. "That would involve looking around to decide and I don't want to lift my head. Your cheek feels like a flower petal."

He rubbed his against it and made a deep, dangerous sound in his throat. The smooth, suedelike feel of a clean-shaven jaw rubbed against her cheekbone made her scalp ripple with feeling.

"I remember," he said quietly as he leaned her backward in a dip, "that you feel like that everywhere."

Helplessly suspended, trusting him completely, she looked into his eyes and saw the danger she'd seen that night, the fatal blend of sweetness and passion that had beckoned to her and made her reckless. That night she'd had only herself to answer to. This night, that had changed.

She used a firm grip on his shoulder to pull herself upright. A mild cramping in her abdomen sent a ripple of discomfort across her eyes. She stood still a moment, steadying herself.

Sin lifted her chin in his hand, frowning. "What is it?" he asked.

"You've had your dance," she replied, feeling fine once again. She must have moved too quickly. "Now, I have to go."

He kept a hold on her chin, his eyes still roving her face. She looked pale, and he thought he'd seen a wave of pain cross her face. Or was he just looking for an excuse to keep her there?

She smiled up at him, suddenly as carefree and remote as she'd been that morning she'd walked out of his bedroom. "It was good to see you again," she said, offering her hand. He suspected it was a deliberately perfunctory phrase intended to make him let her go. She didn't know him very well.

He ignored her hand and took her arm, walking her to the little group where Rebecca stood.

Bobbi felt light-headed and disoriented. Something was tightening again in her stomach, and she didn't want to consider what it might be. It was just a quiet discomfort now. She told herself she was being foolish, that she'd eaten a very sweet piece of cake on an almost empty stomach and it was simply a sign of indigestion.

She forced a smile for Rebecca, thanked her for inviting her and told her how much she'd enjoyed meeting her friends.

"Do you have to leave so soon?" Rebecca complained, walking them to the door.

"Sin isn't leaving," Bobbi said, smiling up at him, daring him to contradict her.

"I'm walking her out to her car," he said, putting an arm around her shoulders to sabotage any resistance.

"Oh, Parsons will get the ca—"

Sin silenced Rebecca with a smile and stopped her butler with a shake of his head. "We can manage," he assured them. "I'll be right back."

Rebecca returned his smile. "Of course. That's all right, Parsons."

"*I* can manage," Bobbi whispered to Sin as he walked her slowly down the circular driveway. "You don't have to follow me."

"I'm not following you, I'm accompanying you," he said.

"Either way, I don't need you." It helped her to say it. It just didn't help her believe it.

"I think you do," he corrected her mildly, "or you know you would if you gave yourself the chance. That's why you're running out early, isn't it? That's why you don't want to be friends."

The tension was tightening in her stomach and she concentrated on it for a moment, praying that it was just nerves.

"You have no answer for that?" Sin asked, keeping pace with her as she quickened her step.

"'Fraid not," she said, longing for the security of her little car, wanting desperately to be out of beautifully gardened Beverly Hills and away from gorgeous Paul Sinclair. She'd feel better in her apartment. She knew she would.

She stopped by the driver's side door of her car and delved into her tiny bag for her keys. The gripping pain suddenly closed over her like a fist, causing her to gasp and lean forward, dropping her purse.

"Bobbi!" Sin caught her against him.

The pain was gone in an instant and she drew a ragged breath, working to keep the panic out of her voice. She laughed nervously. "I have an ulcer that kicks up," she said.

He frowned down at her in the dissipated glare of the lawn light. "When we visited Candle Bay, you ate Cajun food. What's really wrong, Bobbi?"

"An ulcer," she insisted, pushing out of his arms and standing on her own to lend credence to the phony smile she gave him. "I didn't have it in May." Mercifully she'd retained a hold on her car key. She forced it into the lock, now desperate to get away from Sin. It wasn't going to happen this way. It wasn't.

He picked her purse up off the street and caught her arm before she could slip in behind the wheel. Her cat's eyes were glazed with pain and anguish.

"You're not driving home," he said, taking the keys out of her hand.

"Don't you tell me..." She made a snatch for her key ring but he held it up beyond her reach.

"I'm taking you home," he said, "or you're going back inside to lie down."

"I'm not going back inside!"

"Then, come on." He caught her arm and tried to pull her toward the shiny Porsche convertible at the end of the driveway.

"Sin, I won't..." This time the pain ripped across her abdomen and made short shrift of her attempts to delude herself into believing she wasn't in serious trouble.

With a cry of pain she sank to her knees, or would have if Sin hadn't caught her.

"Okay, that's it!" he said angrily, swinging her up into his arms. "We're going to the hospital." He ran her to the Porsche, knowing it'd make the five blocks in under two minutes.

He placed her in the passenger seat, yanking the seat belt over to tie her in place. She gulped in a breath as the pain abated.

"Oh, God," she said as he leapt behind the wheel without opening his door. "I don't want to lose it."

"Lose what?" he asked, not even looking her way as he concentrated on putting the key into the ignition and the car into gear.

"My baby," she said in a strained voice. "I think I'm having a miscarriage."

Chapter Two

In the hospital waiting room, corny dialogue came from a television at the other end of the room, and someone across the hallway laughed on the telephone. Sin checked his watch. It was just after eleven o'clock. It seemed like an eternity ago that he and Bobbi had danced.

He got up and paced to the window. He could still see the desperate look in Bobbi's eyes. And, finally, he'd understood.

"Mr. Perducci?" a voice asked behind him.

He turned to face a husky balding man with glasses and a questioning smile. A badge on his lab coat said he was Dr. Britain.

"No, Sinclair," he corrected, offering his hand. "How is she?"

The doctor shook hands with Sin and nodded reassuringly. "Pretty well. Come on into my office and I'll explain everything."

Almost painfully relieved, Sin followed him down a corridor covered in children's artwork and into a small office furnished in green plastic chairs with steel frames. Bobbi, Sin thought absently, would be horrified by them.

Britain closed the door, gestured him to a chair and took his place at a small metal desk cluttered with papers and medical paraphernalia. He looked at Sin over his glasses.

"You're the father?"

Sin had had a tense hour and a half to put that answer together. "Yes," he replied.

Dr. Britain removed his glasses and turned in his chair to face Sin. "What's happened to Barbara is frightening, but common enough that it's easily remedied in most cases."

For an instant Sin was confused. Who was Barbara? Then he realized it must be Bobbi's given name.

"It's called preterm labor," Britain went on. "For reasons we can't always explain, the cervix becomes confused about what it's supposed to do and tries to deliver the baby early—sometimes, as in this case, long before term. I've given her magnesium sulfate to stop contractions and she's responding."

"Then, the danger's over?"

"For the moment," the doctor replied. "We never know for certain if the problem is solved for the duration of the pregnancy. Often women who go into preterm labor this early will do it again. I'll prescribe a medication she'll have to take four times a day. I'd like to keep her overnight."

"But, she's all right?"

The doctor smiled. "She must be a very strong, independent woman. Once we assured her the baby was safe, she was more upset by the fact that she couldn't stop crying than that she'd been in pain."

Sin nodded and stood. "Yes. That's an apt description. Can I see her?"

"For a few minutes. Come with me."

The doctor led him through double doors and down a side corridor, then into a room with two beds. He pointed to the bed near the window, cautioned him to remember that she was exhausted and disappeared.

Sin walked quietly past the woman asleep in the first bed, and went to stand over Bobbi, staring at him from the second. She was attached to a machine that apparently recorded some function of her body. She looked startlingly pale and frail within the confining bars of the side of the bed.

"Hi," he whispered. She raised her free hand as though to touch the hand he placed on the rail. Then she changed her mind.

He readjusted the blanket she'd disturbed. "How do you feel?"

"Pretty good now. They've given me all kinds of things." She smiled thinly. "Thank you, Sin."

"For getting you in the condition that brought you here?" he asked softly.

She looked him in the eye. "You're presuming things you don't know," she said. "I never said it was *your* baby."

He looked back at her. "I'm smarter than I look."

"Well," she said, squaring her shoulder against the bank of pillows and clearing her throat, obviously trying to look in control of the situation, "the baby's okay now, and there's no more need to worry. I'm going to be fine. This doesn't change anything. This is *my* baby, and if you're feeling possessive and responsible, I assure you I'll take excellent care of him and I free you of all obligation toward either of us. I'll even put it in writing if you like. I'm sure an attorney would like everything to be legal."

Sin let a full half minute tick away while telling himself that she'd just been through a traumatic experience, and that she was under medication that was probably affecting her thinking.

"We'll argue about this," he finally said calmly, "when you're discharged."

"We won't argue about this at all." She paused to yawn, then went on with an edge of drowsiness in her voice. "I appreciate your getting me here, but you have nothing more to do with this."

"Get some sleep," he said, straightening away from the bed. "I'll see you in the morning."

"Sinclair..."

He put a finger to his lips. "You'll wake the other lady. Good night." He paused at the door to wave, then closed it behind him.

A sleepy voice came from the depths of the other bed. "Don't burn your bridges, honey. You're going to need him."

"WHERE'S MY LANDLADY?" Bobbi asked as Sin lifted her out of the wheelchair. He put her into the passenger seat of a blue-and-silver Blazer and waved the nurse off with a polite thank-you. "I asked the nurse to call her to pick me up. And where's your Porsche?"

He climbed in behind the wheel, checked the rearview mirror and backed out of the parking spot. "Your landlady was busy, and I thought you'd be more comfortable in this than in the Porsche."

It was a bright, sunny day, all southern California had to offer at this time of year. Somewhere to the north and east, summer would be slipping toward fall. Though she'd lived her entire life in the sunny west, Bobbi always felt autumn inside her, as though her internal clock ignored her seasonless surroundings.

She smiled as she thought that now her clock had other duties. Thoughts of her baby made her turn to Sin. The sight of him filled her with a curious trepidation. She wasn't sure why, unless it was his abrupt, purposeful movements, the rigid set of his jaw. His usually smooth grace seemed to have been altered by an almost military set to his head and shoulders, and the mouth that grinned and laughed so readily appeared to have forgotten how today.

She'd just been confined too long, she told herself. Almost thirty-six hours in bed had felt like a month in prison. Her mind was already turning with the hundreds of tasks waiting for her in her shop.

"I can't wait to get home," she said as he pulled out of the lot and onto the highway. "I've got a million things to do. I'm working on a Shaker bench I found at a flea market in . . ." She went on in detail about the bench, assuring herself that Sin's silence indicated rapt attention.

By the time Sin reached the freeway, Bobbi had run out of chatty detail.

"What was Mrs. Grabinski doing today?" she asked.

"Who?" he asked absently as he flipped his turn signal and watched the side mirror.

"Mrs. Grabinski. My landlady."

"Ah . . ." He merged with the traffic onto the on-ramp, then slipped smoothly into the speeding traffic. "Something to do with her daughter."

"I thought her daughter lived in Tucson."

Sin shrugged while watching the road. "She must be visiting."

"And where are you going today?" She took the fabric of the sleeve of his navy-blue-and-white rugby shirt between her thumb and forefinger. "Obviously not to the office."

He shook his head, still concentrating on the road. "I have a cabin in the Willamette Valley in Oregon where there's great fishing."

"Is that anywhere near Patrick and Gina?"

"About eighty miles over a beautiful mountain range."

Well, good for him, she thought. She had her own fish to fry. She'd started to make plans last night in her hospital bed. There'd be no more skating by for her, taking just the jobs she enjoyed doing so that she could give them the time they deserved. She had to actively acquire more clients, make good use of those she'd met through Rebecca, maybe rent space in an antiques mall where she could sell the work she did on the side. Maybe she could find a small house to rent. Something with a yard and a fence.

She watched Sin move into one of the lanes that led to an interchange. She was glad he wasn't arguing with her about her decision to care for the baby by herself. Though he'd insisted the night before last that they'd discuss it today, he seemed to have changed his mind.

She liked to do things her way, and this singular, most important project of her life was something about which she had very specific ideas.

"I want you to know," she said, the beautiful day making her feel magnanimous, "that I'm pleased with your attitude in all this."

He sent her a swift, clear-eyed glance. "Really."

"Yes." She opened her window and leaned out on an elbow to sniff. She couldn't smell fall, but she knew it was out there somewhere. Her short hair fluttered in the breeze. She turned back to face him. "Had you gotten all possessive and bossy and pretended things you didn't really feel, I'd have resented it. It's *my* baby. And the wisest thing you can do for it is to get on with your life and let me get on with mine."

He sent her that look again, but this time said nothing.

She was absorbing the wonder of having spent twenty minutes in his company that morning without argument, when she noticed the overhead signs.

"Sin, you're going the wrong way," she said, pointing over her shoulder.

His wrist resting atop the steering wheel guided the Blazer as he watched the traffic ahead. "No, I'm not," he said.

Her earlier vague suspicions began to take firm, alarming shape. She tried to deny it a little longer. "We're on an errand."

"No," he replied easily.

"Sinclair." Her voice was high with concern and she had to concentrate to keep from shouting. "Where are we going?"

He gave her a quick smile. "Do you fish?" he asked.

Chapter Three

Bobbi determined to remain calm. She wouldn't give him the satisfaction of knowing she was approaching a state of panic.

"No, I do not fish," she replied, "and I do not wish to learn."

"That's all right." He nodded at the road, his tone indulgent as though he were granting her something she wanted. "The cabin's very cozy. You can sit inside and knit or read or something."

"I don't knit, Sinclair," she said with quiet ferocity, "but I am going to read you the riot act if you don't let me out of this car this instant."

He gave her an unconcerned glance that told her he wasn't even remotely affected by the threat. "You're going to Gold Grove, Bobbi. Since flying isn't a good idea for a woman in your fragile condition, it's going to take us a little longer to get there. You may as well resign yourself to it."

She was losing the calm and felt herself bristle. "This is kidnapping."

He shook his head. "Hardly. I'm taking my woman and my child to a safe, warm place."

"I'm not your woman, Sinclair," she said firmly. "Now, let me out of this car."

He glanced at her, that expressive eyebrow clearly telling her he didn't believe that for a minute.

"One night of...of..." She groped for the right word. She still didn't know how to describe or explain what had happened.

"I remember what it was," he said with quiet gravity.

For one long moment silence rang between them.

"We were lonely," she finally said reasonably. "And it was a comfort to have someone to hold."

He inclined his head as though considering. "That's how it started."

She tried a new approach, straightening in her seat to give the appearance of calm control.

"It doesn't matter how it started," she said, studying her fingernails. "The important thing is that it's over. Please take the next off-ramp and let me off. I'll call a cab."

He made no move to switch lanes and she sighed.

"I have a business to run, you know."

"I've taken care of it."

"What?" She sat up and turned to him again, asking warily, "How?"

"I called Gina," he replied, turning the Blazer onto the interchange that would lead them north. "She told me about the man who helps you out sometimes when you're swamped. I got in touch with him, explained the situation and made him a deal he couldn't refuse. He'll keep the shop open for you until you get back.''

''And when do you foresee that will be?'' she asked, about to burst with temper. She could just imagine Fabio Ferrarra, who'd been a friend of her father's and was always telling her she should remarry, being delighted that a man had taken over her life. He'd do everything he could to cooperate.

''After the baby's born,'' Sin replied, now driving at high speed as the northbound traffic merged and moved ahead, unobstructed. ''Giving you a month or two to relax and adjust, I'd say early spring.''

''And where will you be all this time?'' She was sure she knew, but she wanted to hear it from his own lips.

''With you, of course,'' he answered, giving her a smiling glance.

''No!'' She snapped the word at him with all the firmness and clarity of which she was capable, while still determined to maintain control of herself. She was forced to admit she'd long ago lost control of the situation. ''Now I see why you chose not to argue with me. That would have been too democratic! People of your *social strata*...'' She emphasized the words she'd regretted speaking the night before last, but now meant in all sincerity. ''...just do what they damn well please and expect everyone else to fall into line. Well not me!''

She was trying to control her temper... because any minute she would give him a punch in the eye.

He, on the other hand, continued to drive as though he were alone in the car.

"The moment we reach a phone," she threatened, "I'll have you arrested. I'll take you to court!"

He smiled wickedly

"I know you have a reputation for being wily and clever and silver-tongued," she told him, straining against her belt, "but I'd have the law on my side! It's my baby!"

He gave her a regretful glance as the traffic thinned and he moved to the slow lane, setting the cruise control. "Actually many judges believe the father's rights to his baby are equal to the mother's, even when the baby is still in the womb. I recently won a case for a client whose girlfriend tried to deny him visitation rights to their out-of-wedlock baby. The judge ruled in his favor."

She gasped indignantly.

"It's true," he insisted. "You have to come to terms with the fact that the baby belongs to both of us."

Bobbi fell back against the seat in frustration and impotent anger. "I don't want anything from you."

"I'm not giving you anything," he argued quietly. "I'm taking care of my child. I'm afraid as long as you're carrying it, and doing kind of an iffy job of it, you're being taken care of, too."

Offended, Bobbi glared at him. "I've taken excellent care of your child." She heard herself, then corrected instantly, "My child."

He nodded. "I know you're trying, but Dr. Britain says your body isn't sure what it's doing. He wants you to relax, remain calm and keep your space stress free. Gold Grove is the best place to do that."

Bobbi closed her eyes and rested her head back. She was suddenly exhausted. "And what are your plans once the baby's born?"

Sin knew she wasn't ready for that. "We've an awful lot to go through in the next five months. Let's just take things as they come."

She rolled her head on the headrest to fix his profile with a hard green gaze. "You're not taking this baby away from me."

He met her gaze, held it for an instant, then turned back to the road. His profile had softened, she noticed. "Of course not," he said.

Then what's the option? she wanted to demand. But, the only one she could think of she didn't want to hear.

"I'm not giving up," she said as she tried to get comfortable. "I just . . . need a nap."

He worked a few controls on the armrest and her armchair seat tilted back to a comfortable angle. He reached behind his seat and produced a dark blue popcorn-stitch afghan, which he tossed over her, one-handed.

"Thank you," she said grudgingly, adjusting it. She pulled it up to her chin and gave him another glare. "You'd better have all your arguments ready when I wake up, and a good story to tell the judge."

"Right." He didn't sound worried.

"I'm going to make your life miserable."

He didn't dispute that.

"You're going to be sorry you ever met me."

He doubted that, but there were still too many details hanging fire to reach that conclusion.

"Go to sleep," he said.

"Shut up," she said, then did just that.

BOBBI AWOKE, startled by the sudden lack of movement and the silence of the wheels whose hum had lulled her to sleep. She sat up to find Sin watching her, then fell back because of her tilted seat.

He pushed the control and her seat whined quietly back into place. "Food," he said with a smile. "You for it?"

It took her a moment to look around and assure herself that her kidnap had not been a dream.

"Where are we?" she demanded.

"Bakersfield," he replied. "And it's hotter than hell, so the less time we spend sitting in the car arguing, the better off we'll be."

"What am I going to do for clothes?"

"Your landlady packed your things. Whatever you don't have, we'll pick up in McMinnville."

Bobbi folded her arms. "I thought she was busy," she said smugly. "With her daughter who lives in Tucson."

"She was," he insisted. "After she packed your things, I wrote her a check to express my gratitude for her cooperation. When I left, she was on her way to buy a ticket to Tucson."

Bobbi shook her head at him. "You think you can just buy what you want?"

"Bobbi," he said patiently, "all I'm trying to do is buy you *lunch*. It's after one, and you haven't had anything since breakfast in the hospital. That can't be good for the baby. And neither can your state of agitation. Relax, accept the inevitable. If you have demands, you can make them over a sandwich."

She tried a long shot. "The only demand I have," she said, "is that you take me back home."

"Home is ahead of you," he said amiably, "not back. Come on. I get cranky when I'm hungry."

Infuriated as she was with him, she couldn't imagine him cranky. He would probably laugh and joke his way out of every altercation and emerge victorious.

It was just her luck, she thought, bracing her hands on his shoulders as he swung her down to the ground, to make a baby with a man with highly developed senses of responsibility and humor.

"A BOWL OF CHOWDER and a dinner salad?" Sin frowned at Bobbi as the waitress walked toward the kitchen with their order. The girl's blue-and-white uniform reflected the Dutch decor complete with blue-and-white plates displayed on the plate rail that ran around the dining-room wall, to the windmill turning cheerily on the front lawn.

Bobbi downed her water thirstily, then asked, "What's wrong with that?"

"The chowder's high in fat," he replied, leaning back as another waitress poured coffee into his cup, and put a small teapot in front of Bobbi. "And the salad is filling, but has no food value."

Bobbi unwrapped the teabag and dunked it into the pot. "Really?" she asked, glancing up at him as she bobbed the bag up and down. "Are you my dietitian as well as my kidnapper?"

"I bought a book on pregnancy and childbirth yesterday," he said, watching her ritual. When her hand stopped moving, he raised his eyes to hers. She was staring at him with surprise and suspicion.

"And?" she asked.

"And, you're supposed to have your full complement of nutritious calories, plus about three hundred, at this stage, for the baby. How much do you weigh?"

She gasped indignantly. "None of your business, Sinclair."

He glanced quickly over what was visible of her above the table. "About one-forty?" He deliberately guessed high with a straight face.

"One thirty-two," she corrected, annoyed. "For a big-boned woman almost five-ten that isn't too bad."

That eyebrow went up.

"All right, medium boned and I'm closer to five-eight. I have a good appetite. I can't help it."

"Sedentary, moderately active or very active?"

She rolled her eyes. "I don't know. I'm not a slug, but I'm not a squirrel, either."

He did a quick mental calculation. "You should consume somewhere between twenty-two and twenty-three hundred calories."

Her eyebrow went up. "Really? I never eat that much. At least, I don't think I do."

"The book contains a great diet," he said. "We'll put you on it when we get to the cabin."

"Sinclair," she said in exasperation, "I know this hasn't occurred to you, but you've no right to tell me what to eat."

He tilted his head to acknowledge that that might be true. "But, it's my baby, too, and I have a responsibility and every right to see that you don't starve it or fill it full of junk."

She rolled her eyes again. "This food stuff is all a lot of hype. My grandfather who owned a farm and lived on beef, butter, eggs and milk with the cream puddled on top lived to be ninety-three. How many skinny little people do you know who eat right, exercise and die young anyway because of a fate we can't control?"

"So the rest of us should throw sound, proven principles away?"

"Maybe the rest of us shouldn't be fanatic."

"Sorry." The way he said the word, she knew it didn't express apology, but rather regret on his part that he had to disappoint her. "I'm fanatic about everything that's mine. Accept it now. Save us both a lot of trouble."

She grabbed her purse and tried to sidle out of the booth. He raised a foot to the edge of her seat, blocking her exit.

She grabbed her knife and wielded it threateningly. "Would you like to be known as No Toes Sinclair? I will not be separated from my family, my friends and my work by an overbearing bully with delusions of possessive paternity."

"With a butter knife?" Sin asked, reaching across the table to take it from her. He leaned toward her, his foot still in place, and said quietly, "I did a little checking. You have no family left, according to your landlady your only close friend was Gina because you work such long hours you don't have time for them, and I explained that your shop will be very ably taken care of by Ferrarra."

"My work is what I do!" she whispered vehemently. "I will not languish in some primitive woodsy cabin to satisfy your yuppy ideas of how to grow the perfect society baby."

The humor in his eyes finally ignited into temper. "If you mention the words social or strata one more time," he threatened softly, "or any form thereof, I will personally..."

Whatever dire consequence he was about to promise was thwarted by the arrival of the waitress, one arm stacked with Bobbi's chowder, salad and basket of crackers. She placed the ham-and-cheese sandwich with its scoop of coleslaw and slices of melon and orange in front of Sin, then unloaded the other arm in Bobbi's place.

"Anything else I can get you?" she asked helpfully.

"A glass of skim milk," Sin replied with a devastating smile. She hurried off to get it.

"Very wholesome of you," Bobbi praised, putting her purse down and abandoning all thought of escape. The chowder smelled heavenly.

"The milk's for you," he said.

Bobbi settled down to eat, resigned to her fate, at least for now.

"OKAY," Bobbi said. They were getting back into the Blazer after lunch. Sin had unlocked Bobbi's door and held her elbow, ready to help her up into the plush seat. She looked up at him, trying to appear conciliatory and forgiving. "I'll forget this whole thing, if you'll take me home."

Sin closed his eyes on a sigh of mild impatience. She went on quickly. "I have a better understanding of your position now. I understand that you want a part in the baby's life, and I'm willing to grant you that . . . within reason. As long as it doesn't make you a part of *my* life. So, why don't you just head south . . ."

"Do you really think," he asked, looking down at her with a curious smile, "that you'll be able to look into the face of a baby with my eyes every day of your life and not think of me as a part of it?"

That did sound impossible. The thought startled her. "Maybe it'll have my eyes," she said.

He shrugged a shoulder. "Then it would have my hair color. Either way, we're bound forever. And it isn't in my nature to be parted from what is mine."

Though he'd already taken her well over a hundred miles from Los Angeles, she was just now beginning to realize how deadly serious he was. He really was taking her to Oregon, and he really did intend to keep her there until after the baby was born.

She swallowed. "You're getting carried away, Sinclair," she warned.

"No." He smiled, swept her up into his arms and deposited her gently in her seat. "You are," he said, handing her her seat belt. "Buckle up."

Interstate Five was a flat ribbon of road that wound through the fertile valleys of southern California, then through the gold mining towns in the north.

On the busy highway, they passed vacationers from every other western state. Their cars, new or old, were piled with children and luggage, toys and food. They passed trucks laden with the rich produce that would be distributed throughout the United States, and endless miles of the fragrant fields from which they came.

She felt herself mellowing just a little. In a very unorthodox way, she was finally getting what she'd wanted for a long time: to think through her life and plan a more successful course for the rest of it.

There were far fewer options open to her now, with the baby coming. But there were more plans to make than ever before. Maybe a few months of quiet wouldn't be a bad thing. She glanced at the man responsible for this doubtful opportunity and realized how little she knew about him.

"Why a cabin in Oregon," she asked, "when you could probably have a yacht in Monte Carlo?"

"I went home with Patrick to Candle Bay almost every holiday break and summer when we were in college," he replied, his voice warm with the memories. "I fell in love with it. He grew up on the coast, it's in his blood. When he went into the military and I came up on vacations alone, I explored inland and fell in love with the Willamette Valley."

"The Willamette Valley," she repeated thoughtfully. "I remember reading about it in school."

"Wagon trains came west one after another, headed for the fertile farmland of the valley—and some of the best fishing anywhere."

She couldn't help grinning. "Do you really think some men uprooted their families and came west because the fishing was good?"

He laughed. "Absolutely. You once told me you'd go to the ends of the earth to find the right piece of furniture."

She frowned in surprise. She did often say that, but she didn't remember saying it to him.

Correctly interpreting her look of confusion, he answered her unspoken question. "You told me the night we made love. We were wading in the shallows at the time."

She couldn't quite bring the memory into focus, except that she *did* remember how easy he'd been to talk to.

"Well, yes," she said, trying to sound matter-of-fact, "but furniture's substantial, something you can live with day to day and pass on to your kids."

"True, but you have to have spent the afternoon fishing on a beautiful stream, then cooked your catch over an open fire at twilight to appreciate how *that* experience stays with you to enrich your life and those with whom you choose to share it. The glow probably lasts as long as your furniture."

His low, rumbling voice made Bobbi almost see the twilight and smell the cooking fire. She stared at his profile in pleasant surprise. "Why, Sinclair. You're a sensitive man."

He slanted her a wry glance. "Don't tell my clients. Lawyers are supposed to resist being touched by anything but their own client's needs."

"How come you're still single?"

"Because I never got married."

"Cute. Does that mean you don't want to talk about it?"

"It means I don't know."

"Scared?"

She was surprised when he seemed to consider that. She'd expected him to deny fear instantly and vehemently. But, then, she was getting used to him doing the unexpected.

"Maybe, on some level," he finally replied. "Mostly, though, I like to enjoy life, and it's been my experience that women take it so seriously."

She nodded, settling back. "It's the old argument. Men want a woman who is exclusively theirs, children to bear their name—but they want the freedom to run around unfettered while the children are being raised and the woman keeps the household together."

"You're generalizing," he said. "And that's not what I meant."

"It's a disease," she insisted, "of all encompassing proportions. I think it's fair to generalize."

They were still arguing around and about the subject hours later when Sin stopped for the night in Modesto.

Sin pulled up in front of the office door. Bobbi caught his arm before he stepped out.

"Are you getting one room or two?" she asked.

He ducked back into the car to look at her. "One," he said. "I can't keep an eye on you if we're in separate rooms."

"Look..." she said, prepared to argue that pregnant did not mean available.

"One room," he said, forestalling her. "With two beds."

She dropped her hand from his arm and stared at him. Would he never stop surprising her?

The room was elegant and comfortable, and Bobbi immediately sank into one of the queen-size beds, exhausted from the long drive.

Sin tucked her in then went out and returned with grilled chicken with pasta and vegetables and a cup of tea. Though she was on the brink of dozing off, he sat her up, insisted she eat, then produced a cup of frozen yogurt he'd stashed in the ice bucket until she was ready for it.

When they'd finished eating, he left the television on for her and went to take a shower.

She was asleep when he emerged, still propped against the pillows, the remote control in her hand. He gently pried her fingers open and removed it, then reached back to click off the television. He tossed the control onto the bedside table, and slipped a hand under her shoulders to lift her head so that he could slip the pillows down.

He had a quick flash in his mind's eye of himself kneeling over her, full with need and life, and her smiling into his eyes, circling her arms around his neck to urge him down and into her.

What he'd given her that night now lay between them. He put a hand to it, not even resting it on her, but just letting it hover there over the denim, letting the rounded little surface fill his palm. Life.

She opened her eyes, looked at him without focus, then closed them again.

He felt her body in his left hand, and the barest suggestion of the baby's in his right. She'd called him possessively paternal, and he couldn't deny that at this moment. He was responsible for their lives, hers and the baby's, and nothing would separate him from them.

She made a small sound of distress and shifted a leg uncomfortably. The jeans. He should get them off her.

He went to her bag, found a short cotton nightgown and carried it to the bed. Then he lifted the hem of her shirt to unzip the jeans. He saw that she'd left them unbuttoned, and that the two ends of the waistband were just short of meeting.

Stupid, he told himself. He should have realized when he picked up her clothes that the items that were usually comfortable to travel in, like jeans, would no longer fit her.

He tugged them off her, holding silky white bikini panties in place while he worked the jeans past her hips. She fidgeted but didn't waken. He tossed them aside then unbuttoned her shirt, carefully slipping one arm from it, then the other.

Her breasts had plumped a little, he noticed, overfilling the lacy white cups of her bra even though she was lying on her back. He reached behind her to unsnap the bra, pulled the nightgown over her head, then eased the bra off her as he pulled the nightie down.

Feeling as though he'd accomplished a feat of great and challenging proportions, he pulled the blankets up to her chin and turned off the light.

The yearning to lie down beside her was almost overwhelming, the need to not be separated by even the space of a few feet from what was now inexorably his required every bit of self-control he possessed.

She didn't understand what motivated him. She found it difficult to believe what he felt. He understood that, and knew he had to give her room to accept it—and pray that in giving her space he would draw her to him where she belonged.

God, he thought, shedding his clothes and climbing into bed, procreation sure as hell made life complicated.

Chapter Four

"Ah!"

Sin heard Bobbi's little scream despite the thin layer of sleep into which he'd slipped.

He was out of bed in an instant, startled and confused when he reached for her bed in the darkness and felt nothing. Then his hand caught her hip, and he realized she was half in, half out of bed.

"Bobbi, what...?" He caught her arm and pulled her up, reaching for the light with his other hand.

He sat down beside her as she squinted against the glare, obviously only half awake.

She drifted against him, nuzzling her head into his shoulder and stayed there. "Mmm." She sighed contentedly. "Better."

God. Sin considered a long moment and decided there was no alternative. This was not going to be easy. He held her against him and eased sideways onto the mattress, still warm and fragrant from her body. In fact, it was going to be hell. He pulled the blankets over both of them and lay back against her pillows, letting her squirm and fidget until she found that place on his shoulder she'd seemed to favor four months ago and went back to sleep.

She would be furious with him when she awoke in the morning, but it wouldn't do her or the baby any good to fall out of bed again, this time possibly connecting with the floor.

As she flung an arm across his chest and splayed her warm hand against his side, he longed for morning and a cold shower.

BOBBI AWOKE with instant awareness and an uncanny sense of déjà vu. She lay on her side this time, but a strong, male arm held her in a hooklike grip, that hand closed firmly but comfortably over her breast. And to her chagrin, just like the last time, she felt her nipple bead against the warm palm.

She flung the arm and blankets off quickly, and was relieved when Sin didn't stir. The feeble light of early morning filtered around the edges of the drapes as she gathered up her clothes and hurried with them into the bathroom.

Just like the last time she'd found herself in this situation, she had difficulty remembering how she'd ended up in the same bed with him. Then it came back to her when she saw the rumpled blankets on the second bed as she turned to close the bathroom door.

She'd almost fallen out of bed. She buried her face in her clothes, disgusted with herself. Since she'd been a child, one side of her bed had to be against the wall. It was a quirk she had not outgrown.

She remembered being lifted back into bed and finally finding a warm, comfortable spot to sleep.

"Okay," she told herself, putting her clothes on the commode and climbing into the shower. "Today you're going to get it together. You're not going to fight him, because that's useless. You're going to take what he's offering, several months of peace and quiet, and you're going to make the most of it. You're going to become relaxed and serene, you're going to make plans, and—after the baby's born—if he offers you money you're going to take it because you'll be able to do things with it for the baby you probably couldn't do on your own—at least not right away."

She thought that last point through a second time as she adjusted the water and decided it might even require a third thought. She'd gotten along just fine not accepting anything from anybody. Just because she now had a child to consider didn't mean that had to change, or should.

She stepped under the warm spray and turned to let it beat against her shoulders. She put a hand to her stomach and patted. "Don't worry about a thing," she said to the baby. "I've everything under control."

Maybe it would be good, she thought, for the baby to grow inside her within the presence of its father. Maybe it would somehow make up for the time it would have to spend without him afterward. She wasn't sure that computed, but it made sense to her in a curious sort of way.

Deep in thought, Bobbi shampooed her hair, then turned the water off and opened the shower door. She stepped out onto the bath mat, then noticed Sin. He had her jeans and shirt over one arm, and a neatly folded pile of clothes in the other hand. He wore only a pair of stone-colored pants.

She gave a little yipe of surprise and reached past him to grab a bath towel, but came away empty. It was farther than she could reach without taking a step closer to him.

"What are you doing?" she asked, trying desperately not to sound like an outraged virgin.

With a slow, somehow seductive swivel of his upper body, he reached behind him, yanked the towel off the rack, and handed it to her.

He was very large in the small space. She clutched the towel to her and began to shiver.

He flipped on the overhead heat lamp and the little room was immediately oven-warm. He took another bath sheet still folded on the rack and dropped the things in his arms on the closed commode.

"I brought you a pair of sweatpants," he said, turning her around and beginning to buff her back and shoulders with the fluffy towel. "And one of my sweaters. I noticed when I tucked you in last night that your jeans must be uncomfortable now. When we get home, we'll get you some clothes."

Bobbi clutched the first towel as he dried her hips with a few vigorous strokes, then went down one leg, then the other. He tossed that towel aside, grabbed a hand towel and rubbed her hair.

"How do you feel this morning?" he asked.

"Fine," she heard herself say as his firm but not quite rough ministrations wobbled her head from side to side.

He stopped, smiling down at her. She emerged from the towel, feeling as though she'd just been tossed into a dryer.

"You sure?" he asked. "You look a little peaked."

"I'm okay," she insisted on a whisper. She was feeling warm all over, and she suspected it had nothing to do with the heat lamp or the brisk toweling.

"Morning sickness?"

"No. I'm just getting over that."

"Good. Okay, put these on." He handed her the neat pile of clothes he'd brought in and snatched up her jeans and shirt. "We'll get some breakfast and be on the road. If you feel up to it, we might even make home tonight."

He closed the door behind him and suddenly the tiny bathroom was just a hot, humid little cubicle again. She noticed as she pulled on the sweats that the atmosphere had gone flat, like a soda left uncovered. She yanked the loose cotton sweater trimmed in red and blue over her head and stared in some concern at the door, ready to admit where the fizz came from. Sin had put the bubbles in her life at a time when it wasn't wise or safe for her to drink champagne. Figures.

Sin packed the car, trying not to think of the nipple beading in his palm, the long, slender leg easing out of the shower stall, the lean body following it with its gently rounding belly and ripening breasts. He was already frustrated enough.

As though her physical enticements weren't sufficient torture, she had to look at him with wary green eyes in a face too pale to be healthy.

She was keeping him at a careful distance. He was used to being placed beyond the circle, outside the bond that held people together, but he'd never learned to accept it.

Bobbi came out of the bathroom looking a little like a tomboy who'd stolen clothes from her big brother's closet. Layers of excess fleece fabric rippled at her ankles and the sweater hung shapelessly on her, its short sleeves hanging past her elbows.

She did a dramatic turn for him, arms held out. "I hope we're not stopping anywhere elegant for lunch."

He put down the case he was about to carry to the car and went to her.

"Style's an inner thing, isn't it?" he asked with a grin as he rolled up her sleeves.

She couldn't help laughing. "If the outer thing is presentable, style can make the difference between attractive and stunning. But I might be out of my league here."

"I can't imagine you out of your league, Perducci," he said, leaning down to fiddle with the billowing hem of the shirt until he found the drawstring waist of the sweats. He gave it one roll, then stepped back to assess.

Bobbi concentrated on drawing an even breath. She could still feel his knuckles against the flesh at her ribs.

"Maybe we'd better cut off the bottoms," he said. "All that excess stuff is bound to trip you up."

"Then you won't be able to wear them again," she protested.

He gave her an over-the-shoulder smile as he replaced the suitcase on the bed and opened it. "No problem." He delved into a pocket and removed a long knife in a leather scabbard.

Bobbi took a step back. "Jeez."

He tossed it once with impressive competence as he came to kneel before her.

"I only threatened *you* with a butter knife," she said as she felt him pull the fabric away from her leg.

"Just don't move," he instructed, "and they won't be calling you No Toes."

The first rip of the knife yanked at the fabric, and she had to steady herself with a hand to his back. Several more rips and he put the knife down, pulled her socks up over the irregular hem and leaned back on one knee to study the effect.

"You look like something out of a chic sportmen's catalog," he said, offering a hand up to steady her so that she could point her foot out and see for herself.

She looked down at the clothes, then at him. "I look like a woman wearing a man's clothes." She pointed to a raggedy hem of the pants sticking out of the sock. "A man who had a pit bull nipping at his heels."

He tucked the hem in, then looked up at her, a forearm resting on his raised knee. "Are you comfortable?" he asked.

She looked down at the blond ends of his eyelashes, the nice V of his brows, the strong line of his nose and the straight line of his mouth with its quirk of ready humor—and forgot the question.

"Pardon me?" she asked, shifting her weight.

He reached a hand up to flatten it against her stomach. "Are you comfortable . . . here, where your jeans were binding?"

She had to swallow before she could answer. "Uh-huh," she replied. Forming a whole word with his hand on her was too difficult.

"Good." He bent over her again, tapping her left foot to encourage her to put it forward.

She did, then felt the smallest, faintest flutter in her stomach. She tensed, making a small sound of surprise.

Sin looked up in concern. "What?"

She stood still, listening, feeling—but the tiny sensation was gone. Had that been the baby's first movement, she wondered, or simply her own reaction to its father's touch?

Either way, she felt a smile come up from deep inside her and had no desire to hold it back. Life *was* growing inside her, and whether or not that was what she'd felt, the reality of it was exciting.

She saw Sin note her smile with some confusion. She leaned a hand on his shoulder and gestured for him to continue. "Nothing. Just lost my balance. Be careful with that thing, please. I've always thought pedicures were pretentious."

BOBBI WAS FASCINATED with how the scenery changed as they drove on. The highway wound higher and higher into the craggy Siskiyou Mountains, the growth on the roadside changing from dry and yellow to lush and green as the hours passed. Deep valleys fell away into a herringbone pattern of evergreen treetops.

They bought sandwiches at a little market and ate at a picnic table on the side of the road at the mouth of a deep woods. Then Sin pointed the Blazer north again and they crossed the border into Oregon.

They stopped for dinner and gas in Grant's Pass. Sin studied Bobbi across the table as she ate a steaming bowl of stew and dipped the end of a slice of French bread into it. He'd tried to coax her into having the trout or the chicken, but she'd refused, insisting that once he was in charge of getting groceries, she'd probably never have anything she liked.

She was still pale, though she ate heartily, and the big sweater did made her look like a refugee from a famine at the Ladies' Professional Golf Association. She seemed finally to have resigned herself to going with him, and had accepted her fate with surprisingly little whining. She talked very little, but he put that down to her interest in the countryside.

He was glad he'd taken matters into his own hands. Ignoring her pregnancy had never been an option for him, but knowing she hadn't wanted him involved had tempted him to establish a trust for the baby.

She glanced up at him now as she scooped up the last bite of stew with the last chunk of bread. "Never seen an appetite before?" she asked. "Don't women eat in your social stra—"

She stopped before the word was finished, just in time to see him straighten threateningly.

"Let me rephrase," she said quickly. "Are you used to slender women? If you are, you'd better take me back now because I'm going to be a bitter disappointment to you in a couple of weeks, if I'm not already."

"I like my women warm and interesting," he said, picking up his coffee cup. "The shape they come in doesn't matter all that much."

"Good thing," she said, dropping her fork into the empty bowl with a clatter. "I suppose pie is out of the question?"

"Knock yourself out." He gestured for the waitress. "But tomorrow it's the straight and narrow for you." When she raised an eyebrow, he grinned and added. "Metaphorically speaking."

The waitress arrived and he ordered Bobbi's pie and more coffee and tea.

"How much farther to Gold Grove?" Bobbi asked.

"Two hundred miles," he replied. "Getting tired and uncomfortable?"

She frowned at the question. "I haven't done anything for two days. Make that three, counting the one in the hospital. How could I be tired?" She laughed. "And I'm wearing my dapper sweats. How could I be uncomfortable?"

He glanced at his watch. "If we keep going, we won't get home until after ten."

The waitress placed Bobbi's blackberry pie à la mode in front of her, then refilled Sin's coffee cup and Bobbi's teapot.

"I'll be invincible once I've had my pie," Bobbi said, picking up her fork. "You want some?"

He winced and shook his head. "I'm not much for sweets, thanks."

She grinned at him as she stabbed the fork into the ice cream and down into the pie. "Must be why you're pursuing *me*."

She was asleep before they reached Eugene, still a hundred miles from their destination. He tilted her seat back and tossed the afghan over her, smoothing a hand over her hair when she stirred fitfully at the disturbance. She nuzzled into the seat, just as she'd nuzzled into his shoulder the night before, and settled down.

So it hadn't been him, he thought ruefully, just the comfort of something solid under her head. Served him right for thinking she would come to need him just because he wanted her to.

Then she patted her hand along the seat as though looking for something. A little sound of discomfort came from her when she didn't find it. Still asleep, she reached into thin air.

Sin took a chance and caught her hand. Hers closed over his and with a little sigh, she sank deeper into sleep. So, he thought with a sense of satisfaction much broader than the small gesture seemed to warrant, she did need him. He was just letting the wonder of that settle inside him when it occurred to him that the more important question might be, did she *want* him?

Bobbi surfaced from sleep just enough to notice a curious shift in cadence from the movement of the car.

Then she realized she was being carried through a cool, pine-scented darkness.

"Sin?" she asked, only mildly concerned.

"Easy," he replied. "I'll put you down in a minute and you can go back to sleep."

"Where are we?"

He stopped, then sat her down on what felt like a soft, cool mattress. "Home," he said, as he untied and pulled off her shoes.

He tilted her back and swung her legs up onto the bed then pulled a cool, plump coverlet over her.

It wasn't *her* home, she thought with only faintly focused stubbornness. Home was in Burbank. But even in her sleepy state she knew that wasn't true.

She curled into the fetal position, seeking to protect her baby, not herself, and thought that now the baby would mean home to her. No, that wasn't quite the right configuration.

The pillow under her head was deliciously soft and the coverlet so cozy that her mind refused to function and slipped back into dreams. As she drifted off, she felt a heavy but gentle hand on her head. Security overlapped comfort and she slept.

BOBBI WOKE LANGUOROUSLY. Aware of feeling absolutely hedonistic she curled and stretched and felt the soft smoothness of silk against her arms and face.

She opened her eyes to focus on rustic fir beams and a hanging light fixture with six tulip-shaped crystal shades. Where was she? It was déjà vu a third time, and she sat up quickly, searching her memory. For a moment, there was nothing there. Then it came back in form if not in substance. Sin's cabin.

She tossed the covers back and saw that she still wore the sweats and shirt she'd worn yesterday, though her shoes had been removed.

She looked around at her comfortable surroundings. They were rustic in style, though not in actuality. Every simple country line of the oak dresser, trunk and desk and chair in the corner spoke of craftsmanship and care, and she knew the fat brass bed in which she sat bore a high price tag. The room, with its vanilla-colored walls, had homespun curtains and a bedspread and chair cushion in country red and blue.

The coziness embraced her. Home was a good word for it, all right, she thought as she swung her legs out of bed. But she knew better than that. Atmosphere wasn't fact. She always had trouble remembering that. Her own passion for family and permanence led her to create things in her mind that weren't really there.

She padded across the pine floor in her bare feet, finding a bathroom decorated in the same colors with an old claw-footed bathtub and a maple counter with a country blue sink. Wall lamps with paper shades flanked both sides of a federal-style mirror.

She headed downstairs, wondering if this were real. *Had* she been kidnapped by the father of her baby, taken from her adequate but simple little house with its attached shop to the lap of rustic luxury?

Arrival at the bottom of the stairs into an old-fashioned living room of large proportions only confirmed her suspicions. The wall of brick that ran under the stairs had an oak mantel the entire length of it topped with lead soldiers from every period of history. A musket hung above it with a powder horn hanging from its stock. Above the bricks to the roof-line were the whole logs from which the cabin was made.

Two wing chairs covered in a red and blue medallion pattern flanked both sides of a wood stove tucked into the fireplace. A bright red wooden settee was placed against the stairs with a quilt over its back, and across the room a very plain Shaker-style table was surrounded by ten spindle-back chairs. A dresser she recognized as probably dating back to the nineteenth century held a collection of pewter plates, tankards and flatware.

She looked around, openmouthed. She hadn't imagined Sin as a collector of antiques.

"A lot of it is stuff my mother has collected," Sin's voice said from behind her. She whirled in surprise to find him standing in a doorway beyond the stairs that led into the kitchen. "She didn't have room for it in any of their places, so she foisted it on me when I took over this one."

Bobbi shook her head in wonder. "It's . . . perfect." She touched the marked and pitted but glossy Shaker tabletop. "The beauty of things from the past, combined with the comfort of pieces you can live with, is the ideal combination. It's what I look for in my work."

"Then you'll feel at home here." He leaned against the doorway molding, wearing jeans and a blue USC sweatshirt. Something about him both drew her and kept her at a distance. "Ready for breakfast?"

She asked suspiciously, "Grapefruit and granola?"

"Whole wheat pancakes with apples," he replied, tossing a dish towel he held over his shoulder and turning back into the kitchen. "Come on."

Breakfast was delicious. "You're a good cook, Sinclair," she praised, chasing the last raisin around her plate with the tine of her fork. "What's for lunch?"

"I'll let you wonder," he said, pouring her another cup of juice.

The kitchen was brick with a wall of oak cupboards, new appliances and antique cabinets. The far wall was a sliding glass door onto a deck where she could see twig furniture. Beyond it was a thick, green woods through which sunshine streamed.

They sat at a round table surrounded by a motley collection of old chairs in the middle of the room. The room was enormous and airy despite the brick, and made Bobbi feel as though she could sit in it for hours over coffee and good conversation.

She straightened in her chair to shake off the homey mood that tried to settle over her again.

"We have to talk about a few things," she said in an authoritative voice, pushing her cup aside and fixing her gaze on Sin.

He sat opposite her with his fresh cup of coffee, his chair pushed back from the table, one ankle angled on the other. "All right."

She had his complete attention, and for a moment that unsettled her. Then she leaned toward him on her folded arms. "I am a free human being," she said, pointing a finger back at herself.

She paused, giving him the opportunity to agree, if not verbally, at least with a simple nod. He didn't. It was not a good start.

"You take issue with that?" she asked coolly.

"On two points," he said. "Firstly, I think freedom is a myth. It doesn't exist. Everyone strives for it, but no one ever finds it. You always owe someone, if not financially, then emotionally. No matter how you try to remove yourself from the cycle of give and take, you find yourself in there somewhere, either with someone needing you to give to them, or you owing them because they gave to you."

She stared at him a moment, off balance by the philosophical turn her simple statement had taken.

He grinned and sipped his coffee. "But for the sake of argument, if you consider your single status as freedom, I don't think you're as much *free* as you are simply... adrift. Hurt by a relationship, afraid to take a chance on another."

She continued to stare. His grin broadened and he lowered the cup to his knee. "But do go on."

"I hope," she said in a kind of fascinated annoyance, "that you explore your own psyche as closely as you seem to have examined mine."

"How do you think I reached that conclusion?" he asked. "We have a lot of the same hang-ups. We're more alike than you realize. But, continue. You are a free human being. What follows?"

"The point I was trying to make," she said in exasperation, "is that I've let you bring me here because on the road, there was little I could do about it. Now, the situation is different."

"How so?"

"There's a telephone right there," she said, keeping her voice calm while pointing to the antique crank device on the wall. "You can't watch me every moment. I could have the police here in..." She faltered, not sure how far they were from a town. "In no time," she went on nonspecifically. "You'd be behind bars as quickly."

Again, she waited for him to indicate that she was right. He didn't. She drew a breath and knew she'd hate herself for asking, "You disagree?"

He sipped his coffee. "On two points," he said, placing his cup on the table. His blue eyes met hers with amiable evenness. "Firstly, your landlady and your employee willingly made it possible for me to bring you here, and your best friend, Gina Gallagher, will tell anyone who asks that you came willingly. She sends her best, incidentally. I talked to her early this morning."

For a moment, Bobbi couldn't speak. She was simply too annoyed to be coherent. Then finally she reminded him, "I thought you had a second point."

"I do," he said. "That phone's not connected. If you have to make a call, use the one in the living room, or in my office upstairs. There's also a cordless one in your workshop."

It was a moment before the words registered. She watched him pick up his coffee cup and take another sip before his statement dawned on her.

"My what?"

"Your workshop." He put the cup down again and smiled at her. "Want to see it?"

"No, I don't want to see it," she said, barely keeping herself under control. She pushed her chair back with a scrape that made her feel for the flooring but gave her great satisfaction. She walked around the table to glower down at him. "What I *do* want to see, is some evidence in you that you're not going to spend the next five months trying to dictate my diet and my every move. I am the mother of our child, but I have no other tie or responsibility to you! Is that clear?"

She was leaning over him now, one hand on the table, the other on the back of his chair. Their noses were an inch apart. He didn't flinch.

"Is that clear?" she repeated quietly.

For a moment she thought she had him. He looked back at her, the nonplussed laziness in his eyes altering slightly to sudden attention.

Then his hand whipped out from his knee where it lay to cup the back of her head and bring her down to him that extra inch. His mouth covered hers as his other arm closed around her waist and pulled her off balance and into his lap. He leaned her backward over that arm and kissed her senseless, softening her instinctive stiffness with mobile, artful lips until hers parted. Then his tongue delved into her mouth and made her crazy.

He finally raised his head and tilted her upright, looking indulgently into her stunned expression. "Do you think," he asked, "that you can recall how our baby was conceived and be able to convince yourself that we have no tie or responsibility to each other? You feel something for me already. I feel something for you.''

Trapped in the crook of his arm, she felt every nerve-ending in her body riot.

''You're feeling guilt,'' she said, trying not to struggle in his hold, but determinedly looking over his head to the glass door and the deck and woods beyond. ''I'm feeling . . . cozy.'' She said the word as though it were something evil.

He rubbed a hand gently up her arm. ''Cozy?'' he asked, obviously confused.

She shook his hand off and stood. ''Cozy!'' she shouted at him with the same inflection she'd used before. ''It gets me every time. And what do I get? A few men passing through my life whose idea of a cozy evening is a beer and a football game.''

''I am loyal to the Rams. I guess nobody's perfect.''

''Sin,'' she said patiently, ''this isn't going to work.''

''You just said you felt cozy.''

''It's this house.'' She looked resentfully around the kitchen. ''It's so warm and wonderful.''

He studied her a moment, then shifted his weight and folded his arms. ''You're telling me,'' he asked with a tone of uncertainty, ''that you don't like this house because it's warm and wonderful?''

She gathered up their dishes and carried them to the sink. ''I'm telling you I do like it. That's why I don't think I can stay.''

He turned her around and leaned her against the counter, planting a hand on either side of her to hold her there. "Make me understand that," he said in a challenging tone.

She rolled her eyes. "I would end up wanting to stay here."

Sin felt a small flicker of hope under the awesome concerns and responsibilities. He tried not to let her see it.

"And that would be impossible," she added.

"Why?"

"Because we have nothing in common but a baby."

"You keep saying that, but you don't believe it. Every time I kiss you, I get another message entirely."

"Yeah, well your kisses..." She pushed at him ineffectively, "are what got us into this in the first place. You refuse to see me as a free woman, and I refuse to belong to you. We'll only make each other miserable for five months. Take me to the bus station and put me on a southbound."

"Barbara Elizabeth," he said with strained forbearance, "you're angry at me because I won't let you lie to yourself." He opened his hand against the slight protrusion of her stomach. "You have my baby in here. That makes us as close as a man and a woman can possibly be. You're not going anywhere. You're going to stay here and nurture this child, and enjoy this warm and wonderful house, and get to know me. And if you promise to stop talking about how it is not going to work, and how you want to hop a bus, I will let you see the couch thing in the shop."

She had to struggle through the all-encompassing sensation his hand created on her stomach to focus on the words he'd spoken.

"A couch thing?" she asked.

"I don't know," he replied. "All Gina told me is it's eighteenth century. It looks a little like something my mother has in the London house. Want to see it?"

She looked up at him, unwilling to admit an overwhelming desire to know what the "couch thing" was. No antique furniture junkie in her right mind would pass up the opportunity to see an eighteenth century anything.

"You still refuse to admit that I'm free?" she asked.

"I'll admit that you're unattached," he said.

It was no concession at all, but she did want to see his surprise. At least, that's what she told herself when she allowed him to lead her to the workshop.

Chapter Five

Bobbi gasped at the battered little love seat sitting under a work light in the shop. The wood, which she guessed to be pine, was dry and rough and the old flowered upholstery on the seat was threadbare. But the natural grace of its design and construction was visible through its woebegone appearance.

It had a slightly rougher look than the expensive collectibles it copied, and Bobbi guessed some gifted Sunday-afternoon carpenter had made it for his wife or sweetheart.

"This 'couch thing,'" she said, kneeling before it to run her fingertips over the wood, "is a twin-chair-back settee."

"Looks just like two chairs," Sin said, "except there's no middle arm."

She grinned at him. "Nothing to interfere with a romantic gentleman's inclinations."

Before Sin could comment on that, she added in wonder, "I can't believe you did this."

He came to stand over her. "I want you to be happy here. Gina assured me this would help."

She straightened to look around the room finished in corkboard with deep, wide work surfaces running along two walls.

"The man who built this place also built his own boat in here. What else do you think you'll need?"

"Well..." She was giving in fast. She could feel it happening. The capitulation had already gotten away from her like a downhill snowball. The kind man, the cozy home and the settee to work on were too much to fight. "My tools," she said.

He nodded. "I had them shipped. Ferrarra helped me pack the crate."

Indignation tried to surface, but hadn't sufficient strength. It was difficult to be annoyed, Bobbi decided, when everything was being done for you.

"This is very nice," she conceded. "Thank you."

"You're welcome. Come and look outside." Sin beckoned her through the back door and into the backyard.

Immediately to their left were two steps up to the deck with its twig settee and chairs covered in a small blue and brown print. On a low bench was a large carved Canada goose, and an old jug with an American flag on a stick tucked into it. The miniature stars and bars caught the early-morning breeze.

"Does someone live here while you're away?" Bobbi asked, surprised by the little details that suggested habitation.

"A woman in town checks on it for me every couple of weeks. I told her we were coming, and she stocked the cupboards, changed the beds and put out the deck furniture."

Bobbi took one of the chairs that faced onto the lawn. The grass sloped, thick and green, for about a dozen yards where a dense cedar and evergreen woods took over.

"Where do you go fishing?" she asked, raising her face to the soft early sun and the indescribable fragrance of morning.

"Through the woods a little ways. There's a stream filled with trout."

She turned to him, feeling herself already begin to mellow. She remembered their conversation about the importance to the pioneers of furniture and fishing. "That you catch and cook over an open fire at twilight."

His eyebrow went up as he smiled. "You *do* listen when I talk."

"Just because I don't always agree with you, doesn't mean I don't listen." She closed her eyes and leaned her head against the high twig back. "I presume since I'm your captive, nothing is required of me but my cooperation. If you don't mind, I'll just sit out my time right here." She wiggled in comfortably. "If you brought me a drink, I might even take cooperation a step further and be amenable."

"Don't try," he said. "I wouldn't want you to break anything."

She opened one eye to give him a scolding glance, but it required too much effort and it was such a wonderful morning. She closed it again, then felt him sit beside her.

"I thought we'd have something to drink in town," he said, "after we buy you some maternity clothes."

"I've grown kind of used to my bag lady outfit."

"You can use it to work in, but you should have something to go garage-saleing in. Something else for going out to dinner, and for dancing, although I like that little flared thing you had on the night of the party. I think your landlady packed it."

She opened both eyes and looked at him in surprise. "Garage-saleing? You like to do that?"

He shook his head. "Never done it. But Gina assures me that's where you find some of your best stuff. There's a great home improvement center on the other side of town you'll probably enjoy prowling through, too."

"You mean," she said as though she couldn't quite grasp it, "you're willing to spend the day taking me shopping?"

He didn't seem to understand her confusion. "You need clothes. You'll need supplies, I imagine, and whatever else goes into restoring and refinishing."

She stared at him another minute. "Joey hated to go shopping."

With a mild growl he got to his feet and pulled her up after him. "I am not Joey."

She pulled him to a stop as he tried to lead her into the kitchen. They stood toe-to-toe on the deck.

"What about your work?" she asked seriously. "Can you really take the next five months off? Can you just drop everything and live for me and the baby? It isn't practical."

"No, it isn't," he agreed. "But I've never planned my life by what was practical. I do what I want to do. And right now I want to be right here. My staff will take care of things for me. If they have a problem, I'm only a phone call away."

"Is that good business?"

"My concern is a good baby."

She grinned. "You think you can throw back a bad one, like a fish that's too small?"

"If it takes after you," he said, turning her toward the kitchen door. "That's something I might have to consider."

FELICITY WAS TWO BLOCKS long, but as far as Sin was concerned, it had everything they would need for an extended stay. His two-week trips to Gold Grove had always seemed far too short in the past, and though he'd considered staying on several times, there'd always been an important case ready to go to trial, clients who expected his special attention.

This time, his needs came first. Or, rather, those of his child did. And God knew the child's mother needed time to relax and soften if he was going to see the outcome he envisioned.

He found shopping for clothes an interesting experience. In a little boutique he'd never stepped foot inside in the six years he'd been coming to Felicity, he found himself ensconced in a red velvet chair with Bobbi's large purse at his feet.

As the only customer in the boutique at the moment, Bobbi was bustled in and out of a curtained dressing room. She was turned in front of the mirror, presented to Sin, whom the ladies seemed to think should have the right of approval, then bustled back inside.

By the time they got around to dresses, Bobbi was wearing a bare-shouldered pink thing with a short skirt that dropped from under an empire bustline.

She'd looked at herself in it and beamed as she did a turn. Then she looked at the tag, paled and headed for the dressing room.

"No," she said over her shoulder as the ladies fluttered after her. They looked back at Sin in distress.

He went to the curtained cubicle, privately amused at the influence they seemed to think he possessed. If they only knew.

He peered around the curtain just as Bobbi dragged the zipper down. She held the loose front to her and studied his reflection.

"You look beautiful in it," he said simply.

"It costs more than my microwave," she whispered at him through the mirror. "The other clothes will keep me just fine until the baby's born."

"What about when we go dancing?"

"We're not going dancing."

"We are."

She rolled her eyes and turned to him. "It'll be like dancing with a driver's side airbag."

He grinned. "I do see the airbag connection," he said. "And it has nothing to do with size."

"Ha, ha!" she said, forgetting to whisper.

He shushed her and she impatiently let the dress drop, snatching up a baggy pink sweater from the pile of things on the bench and punching her arms into the sleeves then raising it over her head.

"You're not going to *buy* this baby," she said under her breath, pulling the snug jewel neckline over her head. She emerged from the cotton knit, hair atumble, to find herself backed into a corner, Sin's tall, square-shouldered presence blocking her there.

"What?" he demanded ominously.

She could not remember ever having seen such still anger. It filled the tiny cubicle and made her realize that even the most patient man had a line that couldn't be crossed.

Conscience, not fear, made her apologize.

"I'm sorry," she said, eyes focused on his shoulder. "Since the night you took me to the hospital, you've left me few choices—except the choice to hurt you." She looked up into his eyes. "That was small of me and I'm sorry, but you leave me powerless to fight you in any dignified way."

It took a long moment for the anger to die in him. He looked evenly back into her apologetic but steady gaze and finally drew a deep breath, the taut lines of his face relaxing.

"All right," he said, taking her hand so that she could step out of the puddle of pink taffeta. "We'll forget the dress.'' He reached down to pick it up and toss it onto the pile of clothes.

He turned to push the curtain aside, but she stopped him with a hand on his arm.

"I like the dress," she said softly. "But it's the last thing you're going to buy me. Agreed?"

He didn't.

She leaned her weight on one bare leg. "I'll bet you disagree on two points," she said, fighting a twitch at her lower lip.

"You need a coat and a hat," he said.

When she groaned, he asked, "Is it my fault it snows around here and all you have are southern California clothes?"

She wanted to point out that it was his fault *she* was around here where it snowed, but she decided they'd tangled enough for one morning. And she was getting tired of losing.

With a red swing coat and a red-and-green plaid hat and scarf in a box added to the stack of other boxes and bags, Sin and Bobbi went back to the car.

Closing the trunk on their purchases, Sin pointed to the cappuccino bar across the street. "Ready for a break?"

Bobbi laughed in surprise. "Small town doesn't necessarily mean small style does it?"

"Of course not." He caught her hand, waited for the only car on the road to pass, then walked across. "They have the best scones with lemon curd you've ever tasted."

"I've *never* tasted lemon curd."

"Then you're in for a treat."

Two hours later, after going to the home improvement center, and buying supplies, Sin made turkey sandwiches for lunch and served it on the patio. Bobbi picked up a curious chip from a small pile beside her sandwich.

"My potato chip is blue," she said in some concern.

He poured her a glass of lemonade from an icy pitcher. "It's a corn chip made with blue corn," he said. "No salt, and it's baked."

She bit cautiously and chewed. It was good. "How'd you get to know so much about food, anyway? Did you change midstream in school from culinary arts to law?"

He shook his head as he chewed a bite of sandwich, then swallowed. "My parents were gone so much when I was a kid that I spent a great deal of time in the kitchen with our cook. I can even make candy."

She stopped, another chip halfway to her mouth. "Fudge?" she asked.

"Yeah."

"Penuche?"

"Sure."

She tried not to sound too eager. "You think you'll make some while we're here?"

"Depends." He toyed with his glass of lemonade and looked studiously across the lawn. "Fudge is kind of special. A sort of reward."

The silence beat one second, two, three. "You mean I have to earn it," she said.

"Yes."

"I suppose you have specific guidelines I should follow?"

He knew what she thought, and enjoyed puncturing the suspicion. "Of course not." His quick sip of coffee didn't quite hide his grin. "I'm sure leaving you to your own devices would prove far more interesting."

She leaned back in her chair to study him, surprising herself with the thought that life had gotten more interesting since he'd shouldered his way into it. But it wouldn't be wise to let him know that.

"For you or for me?" she asked.

"Oh, both of us." He put his cup down and turned in his chair to lean an elbow on the back of it. Bobbi got the full impact of his smiling amusement. "From the moment we met, through that delicious night of the wedding, until now, I've found you full of surprises. And this time..." He expelled a chuckle as though holding it in one more moment would have been fatal. "This time, you'll be sober enough to surprise *yourself.*"

She felt the blood rush to her cheeks. She knew it. She'd done something worthy of blackmail on that infamous night.

She asked reluctantly, "How *did* my shoe end up in your sailing trophy?"

His smile broadened as he assumed a thoughtful pose, head thrown back, eyes unfocused. "It was all part of a very exotic dance."

"Dance?" she repeated flatly.

"Yes. You were very taken with the mask over the fireplace. You said it reminded you of your ex-mother-in-law."

"Oh, God," Bobbi muttered.

"You climbed onto my shoulders to hook the shoe on the masks's ear, saying it was representational of the kick in the posterior you'd always wanted to give her."

She groaned, and put a hand over her eyes.

"You lost the other one when you insisted we drink our champagne from my sailing trophy. It signified charting a new course in your life, or something."

Bobbi could imagine her intoxicated self free of the protective inhibitions because of too much champagne.

"How did my shoe get in it?" she asked, lowering her hand, determined to know every grisly detail.

"You wanted me to drink champagne out of it, but decided at that moment that you wanted to do something else entirely. So you put it all away very tidily." His grin broadened as he looked away for a moment then back at her. "And you dragged me, kicking and screaming, into the bedroom."

She gave him a vicious swat on the arm, barely biting back a grin herself. "You lie!"

He raised a hand as though to swear. "It's the truth. You're quite the little siren when your blood alcohol level is high enough."

"And I suppose you did nothing to encourage that?"

"I didn't have to. Once you discovered what a good listener I am, you talked and drank until you suddenly felt like dancing. I've explained what happened after that.''

She fixed him with a judicious stare. "And I don't suppose it once occurred to you to stop me."

He stared back seriously. "Not once."

"You should be ashamed."

"I'm shameless."

He was exaggerating, of course, but he wasn't lying. Still, he wasn't solely to blame for what happened that night. In all conscience, she could only take indignation so far.

She pushed her chair back and fixed him with a friendly smile. "Well, as far as I'm concerned, you can lose your fudge recipe. I will not be entertaining you again with more of my drunken comedy surprises."

He caught her hand as she stood and pulled her down onto his lap.

"You don't understand," he said, holding firm when she tried to push against him. "It wasn't your intoxication that was a pleasant surprise, but the hot little number inside you that you let free when you've had one too many." He frowned in apparently genuine confusion. "Why do you keep such a tight lid on her?"

"How many shoes do you think I can afford to leave in trophy cases?"

Sin looked into her eyes, trying to read if it was fear of herself that kept the passion hidden, or fear or something else—or someone. He couldn't tell. She'd have to be the one to tell him, and she didn't look as though she wanted to discuss it.

"Okay, here's the deal," he said. She rolled her eyes and he held her a little tighter foreseeing an escape attempt. "One kiss, and I'll make a batch of penuche that'll be ready after dinner."

She tried to stand. He held her down.

"I don't want to kiss you," she said gravely, looking him in the eye. Then she burst out laughing. She wasn't sure why.

"Uh-huh," he said, laughing with her. "The jury is not convinced. Just plant one square on the lips. You don't have to get ardent, or anything. Just kiss me."

She leaned an elbow on his shoulder and gave him a wry look. "What's the point of a kiss if it isn't ardent?"

"A kiss doesn't have to be about passion every time," he said, the hand that had held her shoulder now moving to run lightly up her neck and into her hair. "It can express tenderness, satisfaction, apology, happiness."

Gooseflesh rippled along her scalp. "And what," she asked, her voice a little breathless, "would you like expressed?"

"Whatever it is you're feeling."

"Can one convey frustration with a kiss?" she asked, thinking she was being clever.

He turned it back on her by putting his lips to hers with a quick, hard kiss. Then he pulled back and smiled. "That do it for you?"

Her heartbeat had stepped up. She raised a cool eyebrow. "I'm not sure."

"Then show me," he said significantly, "how you would do it?"

She was so filled with frustration at that moment, emotional and physical, that she was sure it would convey itself the moment her lips touched his. And it did.

But she hadn't counted on Sin bringing to it his particular brand of charm. He could, she remembered too late, turn anything into a reason to smile.

His warm, playful lips nipped along hers, kissed them open, probed inside with a teasing, inquisitive tongue, then covered them with his until she leaned backward over his arm out of the chair and felt as though not just her world, but her life had been turned upside down. She felt hot and breathless and just a little crazy.

He drew away and righted her, smiling with satisfaction into her eyes.

"I forgot to mention," he said softly, "that there are some couples whose lips turn every kiss into one of passion. We're one of them."

She didn't know what to say to that because she was beginning to believe it was true. And she was losing sight of what she'd hoped to accomplish during this enforced incarceration.

She pushed herself out of his lap and got to her feet. "I'm going to work," she said, tugging with dignity on her new oversize butter-yellow T-shirt.

"Don't you want to know whether or not you earned the penuche?" he asked with a grin.

She raised a superior eyebrow. "I didn't think there was any question," she said, and headed back into the kitchen.

He watched her go, enjoying the little waddle of her slim backside under the shirt. "Amen," he said under his breath.

Chapter Six

Sin's penuche was outstanding. Probably the best she'd ever tasted. She sat curled up in a chair within easy reach of a plate stacked with the delicious fudge, and a cup of blackberry tea. In her lap was a Vogue magazine she'd picked up in town that morning. The subtle sounds of Sin's cleanup could be heard coming from the kitchen.

She was beginning to get suspicious. This was too good to be true. He'd refused her offer to help clear the table or load the dishwasher. He'd insisted she just "rest the baby." No man, she thought, could be this considerate and attentive and not short-circuit.

She was praying that the tools did indeed arrive tomorrow. The life of a pampered harem queen just wasn't for her.

At that thought, a fresh niggle of suspicion rose again. He'd better not think that because she'd agreed to stay, she'd also agreed to a connubial relationship. He'd taken nothing for granted so far—that was, nothing physical, but he might just be trying to throw her off guard.

"Ready?" he asked.

She jumped and looked up. He stood with his hands on his hips and an expectant look on his face.

"Ready for what?" she asked, her tone defensive.

"The walk we talked about during dinner."

"Oh." She put the magazine aside and pushed herself out of the chair. Was it already getting difficult, or was she imagining things? "I have to warn you, I'm a good walker. I can cover Rodeo Drive, both sides, in two hours flat."

He pushed her before him through the kitchen then reached around her to open the back door. "You're that expert, huh?"

"I am. 'Course, I don't have much money to spend. I think buying things is what tends to slow you down."

He laughed as he pulled the door closed behind them. It was after seven, but the sky was still sunny and bright, the air so perfumed with pine and wildflower and the vague scent of water that Bobbi had to stop and drink it in. It filled her like a draught of purity, she thought, a direct infusion from the hand of God.

Sin put an arm around her shoulder and propelled her gently down the two deck steps and across the lawn to the path that led through the trees. "You have to be from southern California," he said, "to appreciate fresh air. I know how you feel. The first time I came to Oregon with Patrick when I was only nineteen, I wondered why anyone chose to live where you could chew air as well as breathe it."

"Because we need the money," she said on a sigh. "And to make it, you have to be where it is. I've thought a million times about moving somewhere else."

"Where?"

"Oh, I don't know." She pointed to the sun moving through the trees as they walked, flashing light like an old moving picture. "Somewhere out there."

"West? You'd have to live on a houseboat. Unless you mean all the way west, like Hawaii."

"I mean past the sun," she said, dreamily watching it follow them. She saw why this place was called Gold Grove even though the trees were all evergreens.

"Ah," he said, "your little hiding place beyond the sun."

She stopped in her tracks, looking up at him in surprise. "How did you know about that?"

He looked surprised that she had to ask. "You told me about it the night we ... the night of the wedding. That you pretend you have a mystical little place out there."

"I did?" She tried to remember, but couldn't. She hadn't told anyone about that, not even Gina.

He nodded gravely. "You asked me to take you there." Then he grinned gently. "Metaphorically speaking, I think."

She remembered clearly the heat and the glow of that night. The warmth that lasted until morning. "And you did," she said, completely unaware she'd formed the words until she heard them spoken.

He put a hand to his heart and lowered his head reverently. "I did. And it's made this earthly life a little tame by comparison."

"It's just a silly notion," she said, walking slowly on, "that helped me keep my sanity when my parents died, then when Joey left. I imagined that my parents weren't gone, they were just... somewhere out there where I couldn't see them. And when Joey turned out to be a jerk, I felt sure that there was a loving, responsible man... somewhere out there."

Sin squeezed her shoulders. "And all the time I was in Malibu, practically right under your nose."

She looked up at him with mild impatience. "You've been kind, if a little too take-charge, and I suppose no one could fault your assumption of responsibility, though I've tried to assure you I'm perfectly capable of handling everything myself. But you're not the right one."

"I'm *the* one," he said with quiet emphasis. "That makes me the right one. But let's not argue that on such a beautiful night. We have five months to discuss it."

"You don't discuss," she said. "You dictate."

He smiled as he held a low-hanging branch out of her way. "I've found it's the most efficient system for getting my way."

The audacity of that remark forced her to smile. "That's shameless," she accused.

He nodded. "I've already admitted that. Come on. Let's pick up the pace just a little bit. You've got to get the blood and oxygen flowing."

"Can't we just go back and eat fudge?" she grumped.

"It's reward stuff, remember," he said, pointing to a root to alert her to it. She stepped over it. "You can have another piece *after* the walk."

She groaned and made an effort to keep up with his quicker pace. "If this baby is born in a Gold's Gym T-shirt, I'm going to be upset with you."

"I thought you already were."

So did she, but she examined her emotions as they hiked down the trail and couldn't find a trace of animosity. The deep green of Oregon fir and cedar and the rich green undergrowth of the woods wrapped her in its serenity and its calming fragrance. She was beginning to hear the soft trickle of water from somewhere up ahead, and the quiet call of birds, different from their loud, excited, early-morning song.

Nature was settling down for the day, and she found herself in curious harmony with it. Maybe it was time for her to settle down, to look her pregnancy in the face and admit that it was going to change her life forever—and that try as she might to deny it, Sin would have a part in it.

The road spilled onto the two or three foot high bank of a stream so clear that even in the waning light, Bobbi could see the rocks and pebbles that lined the bottom.

Sin led her to a rickety old bench sheltered under a cedar. He brushed it off and Bobbi sat, a little surprised at finding the amenity of a seat at the edge of the woods.

"Is this where you sit when you eat the fish you catch?" she asked.

He shook his head and pointed to the bank. "This formality is all in deference to you. I usually sit right there and watch the stream."

"Why do you live in Los Angeles," she asked, leaning forward with her elbows on her knees and watching the water roll past with melodic little riffles and gurgles, "if you love this place so much?"

She turned to look at him and smiled. "You don't really have the money problem thing. I mean, you'd probably have enough to be comfortable if you never tried another case, wouldn't you?"

He nodded, also leaning on his elbows. But his eyes were on the water. "The need to be productive, I guess. I'm happy doing nothing but fishing and reading and walking for two weeks of the year, but I'm not sure I could do it forever."

"Should I point out," she asked, "that you've just committed yourself to doing exactly that for the next five months?"

He turned to her with a deep laugh. "Hardly. I've an urgent mission. Dietitian, personal trainer, procurer of restorable items, stand-in OB nurse . . ."

She giggled and straightened. "You won't have time to fish." She stretched her arms out and smiled up at the sky just beginning to darken to dusk. "Well, if I thought I could make a living here, I'd stay in a minute. Maybe one day I'll do well enough to buy the cabin from you."

That wasn't the way he saw it happening, but he thought it more expedient at the moment to let her dream. They sat in silence for a few moments, then she stood and stretched her back.

"You okay?" He stood beside her, reaching out to rub gently where she probed with a groan in the small of her back. He studiously kept his fingertips from the soft swell of her backside just below.

She rotated her shoulders and sighed. "Fine. Just a little stiff. I guess this will get a lot worse before it gets better."

"It should get better until the last month, anyway, if you just move around a little more. Ready to go back?"

He continued to rub, and she looked at him over her shoulder. "Do I get my fudge?"

"Absolutely."

"Then, let's go."

IT WAS AFTER ELEVEN and Sin knew Bobbi was exhausted. She'd had her fudge and a glass of milk. Curled up in one wing chair while he took the other, she watched TV contentedly.

He glanced up from his book and saw that she could scarcely keep her eyes open as the "Eleven O'Clock News" rolled on. He smiled to himself, knowing what the problem was. She presumed he'd insist on sleeping with her.

He took diabolical pleasure in stretching elaborately, standing and yawning. He saw her wary, heavy-lidded side glance in his direction.

"You want anything before we go to bed?" he asked.

"No," she said, her tone faintly pugnacious, then she added as an afterthought, "Thank you."

"Sure." He reached out to help her to her feet.

She resisted. "I thought I'd watch the news."

"You need eight hours' sleep."

"I'll sleep in."

He shook his head regretfully. "We have to be in McMinnville by nine-thirty for your doctor's appointment."

"My doc—?"

"Dr. Fletcher. OB-Gyn. You'll like him. Your doctor recommended him."

He noted that for a moment, at least, her concern had transferred from the disbursement of beds, to his tendency to take charge.

"You might have consulted me," she huffed as he flipped off the living-room light. The only light filtered down weakly from a night-light in the upstairs hall.

"You were in a hospital bed at the time," he said. "And it just hasn't come up since. Don't worry. He has a fine reputation. I checked."

Bobbi marched up the stairs, one stair ahead of him, grumbling to herself. When they reached the top, she turned to him, her finger raised to scold. "One day you're going to go too far, Sinclair. Then I'm—"

He snaked an arm around her and slipped his other hand into her hair. She went silent and still, her eyes widening with trepidation mingled with excitement.

"Why wait?" he asked softly, then kissed her until his ears rang and she went completely limp in his arms. He stopped only because he remembered the baby needed oxygen.

He leaned her against the wall and watched her eyes open drunkenly to look into his. He saw the enjoyment she'd felt at the kiss play across her eyes. Then, as she came back to awareness, saw her concern over their sleeping arrangements return in earnest when she added the kiss to her other presumptions.

He waited until he saw her straighten her shoulders, and visibly pull herself together.

Then he kissed her quickly, chastely, and pinched her tush. "Good night," he said, and headed off in the direction of his bedroom and office.

Suddenly fiercely awake, experiencing every emotion, Bobbi went to bed, stared in confusion at the ceiling for a full five minutes, then punched her pillow and fell asleep.

"HERE. I'LL TAKE IT." Bobbi tried to relieve the UPS man of his very large parcel.

Sin pushed her gently out of the way. "I'll take it. You sign for it."

Bobbi signed her name, thanked the man with a smile, then turned eagerly to follow Sin as he carried the box containing her tools into the workshop.

He turned the fluorescent light on over the worktable and severed the tape with a pocketknife.

Bobbi pulled out the tools Ferrarra had carefully packed and lined them up on the table. Her hands itched to use them.

That morning the doctor had declared her and the baby in good health, and said that the Brethine she took every six hours seemed to be doing its job. But he cautioned her not to tire herself out, and to take a nap every afternoon. He insisted she should be able to do anything she wanted to within reason, but to stop instantly at the first sign of discomfort or tiredness.

Having her familiar things around her and the settee in the corner waiting to be refinished, made her feel as though she could go on forever. But she knew Sin had other plans. Resisting them suddenly seemed to be more fun than falling in with them.

She smiled at him beatifically. "Why don't you go start dinner? I'll just spend a little while organizing my stuff."

He smiled back. "Why don't you take your nap while I start dinner?"

"Why don't you go fly a kite?"

"Why don't you smarten up and do what's good for you?"

"Working is good for me."

"Thwarting me will not be."

She looked up at him, a hand on her hip. "A threat?"

"A fact," he replied evenly. "I'm here to take care of you and the baby and I'll get the job done. But it'd be more pleasant for both of us if you cooperate."

Despite the antagonism she felt at what she considered his overprotectiveness, she knew he sincerely wanted what was best for her and the baby. In light of that knowledge, she chose not to scream at him.

"Do you think women who work up until their seventh or eighth months get to nap every afternoon in their offices?"

"No," he granted, "but they probably haven't suffered from preterm labor."

She slapped a package of sandpaper strips onto the worktable. "You're a nag," she said.

He accepted the criticism with an almost-proud inclination of his head.

"What *is* for dinner?" she asked as she crossed reluctantly to the kitchen.

"Sautéed prawns," he replied, following her. "Pilaf and asparagus."

"Yum. Any fudge left?"

"You polished it off this morning."

She looked guilty but not penitent. "It's your fault for being so good in the kitchen. I suppose you'll do a bed check, so there's no point in my trying to sneak out of my room like I used to when I was little."

He was about to turn into the kitchen, and she stood three steps up the stairs to the bedrooms. He stopped to look up at her, that wickedly charming smile forming that always managed to make her feel threatened and excited at the same time.

"A bed check," he said consideringly. "Maybe that's something I should consider. Do I get to check the contents of the bed?"

Her body told her that was an interesting idea. Her mind insisted she think again. "I believe you're just supposed to stop in the doorway and make sure there's a familiar face on the pillow."

He frowned. "A dull practice. I think I could improve upon it." He hesitated a moment. She saw longing flash in his eyes, deep and turbulent. Then he drew a deep breath and pointed her up the stairs. "But you need rest." Then he disappeared into the kitchen.

Bobbi lay atop the covers in the comfortable bed and wondered if staring at the ceiling was going to become a habit.

"DO YOU LIKE DOGS?" Sin asked.

Bobbi was resisting the impulse to run the half a butter-flake biscuit in her hand around the plate to capture the little bit of sauce left from the prawns, rice and asparagus she'd devoured.

She looked up from her plate in surprise. All through dinner they'd talked about going garage-saleing when she'd finished the settee to look for other projects. She was startled by the non sequitur.

"'Scuse me?"

"Dogs," he said, pouring more hot water over the teabag in her cup. "Do you like them?"

"Of course," she replied. "Doesn't everyone? Why?"

"Our neighbor called while you were asleep. He has a golden retriever puppy he's trying to place. He saw us in town together yesterday. After years of seeing me come here alone, he figured I'd gone domestic and might want to give the pup a home. What do you think?''

She loved dogs. They'd had one kind of mutt or another all the time she was growing up.

"I like dogs," she said. "But you must know what puppies are like. It's your house. It's up to you."

"For the next six months or so, it's *our* house. What's your vote?''

She felt called upon to point out the practical. "I'd vote yes, but you have to consider the puppy. Do you think it'll be happy in L.A. when . . . this . . . is over?''

A shadow swept across his eyes and banished his good humor. "Do you think you will?" he asked.

She should have been able to give him a cool affirmative. But, she couldn't. After only five days in his company, and only two in this beautiful valley, she felt as though no other life had ever existed.

Then the shadow was gone and he smiled. "But we weren't going to think about after, were we? I'll call him in the morning.''

"HOW OLD IS HE?" Bobbi got down on her knees as about twenty pounds of golden concentrated energy and affection strained against a blue nylon leash to reach her. Long velvety ears flapped and giant paws flailed the air.

John Kliner, Sin's neighbor about half a mile down along the stream, unhooked the leash. The puppy ran at Bobbi, and Sin knelt beside her to absorb some of the impact of the pup's enthusiasm.

"She's three months old," Kliner said. "Name's Buttercup."

Buttercup whined and wagged her tail as she kissed Bobbi's face, then Sin's. She ran around them in a circle, barking furiously, then stood with her front paws on Bobbi's shoulders and licked her from chin to hairline.

"Hmm." Kliner, tall and lean, folded his arms and grinned at Sin. "Looks like the ladies hit it off."

Sin straightened and nodded. The sight of Bobbi with the puppy robbed him of words for a moment. She was laughing as she ruffled the sniffing puppy's ears. Around them were a tall stand of oak trees, and one solitary red leaf drifted to the ground beside her. There was a bite in the air and the smell of wood smoke from Kliner's house.

The moment was perfect, Sin thought. "Puppy's had all her shots?" he asked his neighbor.

"Due for the third one first of next month. Retriever's real good with kids. You'll love her. Raise her right up with the baby."

Bobbi looked up at that, surprised that Sin had told his neighbor about the baby, wondering when he'd had the opportunity. Then she realized he hadn't had to tell him. She was wearing one of the big T-shirts they'd bought her the day before, and it billowed around her in silent announcement.

"Last one of the litter," Kliner said. "Sweet natured, but driving my wife crazy. Too busy."

Buttercup discovered the end of the silky scarf Bobbi had knotted around her neck, and took it in her teeth.

Bobbi tugged on it, and when that only resulted in a game of tug-of-war, she said sharply, "No."

Buttercup sat, ears back, obviously surprised at being denied something. Then Bobbi reached out to pat her head, telling her she was a good dog. Presuming herself forgiven, Buttercup grabbed for the scarf again.

Laughing, Bobbi got to her feet.

"I'll throw in a bag of dog food," Kliner bribed. "And the collar and leash."

Sin looked at Bobbi, that eyebrow raised in question. "What do you think?"

"I think she's great."

"Warn you right now," Kliner said, "she's rambunctious and headstrong. But I know she'll be a good dog."

Something about that made Sin smile. He scooped the dog up, cradled her in one arm and studied her while scratching gently on her chest.

Buttercup's blunt, baby snout sniffed at him as she lay without struggling, front paws curled, back feet large and rabbitlike. Soft brown eyes returned Sin's thoughtful gaze, then a pink tongue flicked out to kiss his chin.

Sin grinned at Bobbi, then assured Kliner, "I have a way with difficult females," he said. "We'll take her."

Bobbi grinned back, unable to deny that.

Buttercup sat in Bobbi's lap for the ride home, then took a sniffing tour of her new surroundings. She sat at the bottom of the stairs that led to the second level and barked.

Sin, carrying the almost full, forty-pound bag of dog food in from the Blazer, snapped his fingers and called her to him. "Private quarters up there, Buttercup. Come on. I'll give you some lunch."

The puppy studied him in perplexity until he opened the bag in the kitchen and she heard the familiar rattle of kibbles being served up.

She ate with enthusiasm, her tail wagging.

Bobbi filled a pottery bowl with water and put it on the floor beside the plastic bowl Kliner had thrown in with the dog food.

"She has a good appetite," she observed, standing beside Sin who leaned against a corner of the counter.

He laughed softly. "A family connection already."

She grimaced up at him and he laughed, hooking an arm around her neck and pulling her to him. "Headstrong and a hearty appetite," he said, kissing her temple. "You have to forgive me for noting a resemblance. Go ahead and spend some time in your workshop. I'll call you for lunch."

She made a pretense of pulling away from him, but couldn't withhold a smile as she disappeared into the room off the garage.

She pulled on the old sweater she'd left in the workshop the day before, and went to work.

Lovingly, slowly, she stripped old paint and stain off the settee, working carefully into turns and patterns and around edges. She'd left the back door open for fresh air, and found her usual trancelike concentration disturbed by the perfumed morning breeze and the sound of happy barking and the deep, quiet notes of Sin's voice.

She forced herself to return her attention to the piece. In five months they would go their separate ways. It was inevitable. She had to fight the added dimension the puppy brought to the pull of the cozy house.

Buttercup was fast asleep in a sunny corner of the deck when Sin served lunch outdoors. It was a little cool, but the sun was still warm, and the fragrance of the beautiful day was too delicious to waste.

"By next week, it'll probably be too cold to do this," he said, placing a turkey sandwich on grainy bread in front of her, along with a fruit salad and a glass of milk. "You warm enough?"

"Yes. Thank you."

She took a sip of milk while looking out over the deep, velvety lawn. Then she noticed the man in jeans, a sweatshirt and a baseball cap working with a long tool in a far corner.

"Who's that?" she asked, putting her milk down as Sin sat across from her with his lunch.

He looked in the direction she pointed. "John Kliner's brother-in-law," he replied.

"What's he doing?"

"Setting fence posts."

She frowned. "It's kind of a shame to fence off this beautiful, natural setting."

He shrugged as though it didn't concern him. "Civilization does bring its refinements."

Her frown deepened. "Say, what?"

"'Bout here?" Kliner's brother-in-law shouted. He'd set one post and had crossed the lawn to the edge of the trees.

Sin gave him a thumbs-up and he waved acknowledgment.

"When it was just me, I didn't need a fence," Sin explained. "But now there's you and a puppy and a baby to think about. My life has to fall into some kind of order. It needs good food and fences."

"Sinclair." She put down the sandwich she'd picked up and looked him sternly in the eye. "By the time this baby is ambulatory, I will no longer be here."

"By the time this baby is ambulatory," he corrected mildly, spreading mustard on his sandwich, "you will be on our second pregnancy."

"I knew it!" She slammed her hand on the table and stood as anger rose the length of her and erupted. "Give a man an inch and he takes a mile! You're all the same. You may have been able to force me to come here, but you will *not* force me to stay."

He looked up at her, apparently surprised by her outburst. "No, I won't force you," he said quietly. "But, it'll happen."

"It won't," she insisted. "Just because I'll have a baby doesn't mean I'll need a man."

"I'm not just a man," he pointed out reasonably. "I'm the baby's father. I thought your own family life meant everything to you."

She hesitated, startled by the argument's sudden turn. "It did."

"Would it have meant the same to you," he asked, "if your mother had run out on your father?"

"That doesn't have anything to do—"

"It does. Would you deprive our baby of what you had when it all meant so much to you?"

Tears, hot and copious, rose out of nowhere to clog her throat, burn her eyes. She ran through the kitchen and the living room and up the stairs, yearning for the privacy of her bedroom. But for once, the solitude didn't help.

Perversely these tears weren't satisfied with simply being shed. They seemed to need comfort and cosseting—notions she'd long ago abandoned. Angry with herself for wanting them, she curled around her baby, determined to cry for five minutes then go back to her workshop.

A gentle rap sounded on her door.

"If you come in here, you'll be sorry!" she threatened.

Intrepidly Sin walked into the room.

She turned her face to the window. "I'll be fine in a minute," she said, her voice husky and heavy. "Just leave me alone."

He sat beside her and put a gentle hand to her hair. "I can't leave you alone," he said. "My job right now is to be with you."

She sniffed. "Consider yourself fired."

"You can't fire me." He tugged on her arm, trying to turn her toward him. "The position of father lasts a lifetime. Turn around and let me show you that having a man looking after you might have a few perks you hadn't anticipated."

She turned onto her back and looked at him without expression, unaware that her damp cheeks said all she was trying so hard to withhold. "Like what?"

He slipped a hand under her back and sat her up. "Like arms to hold you when you cry."

They sat face-to-face in the middle of the bed, knees turned in opposite directions. In her eyes he saw the fight to retain her fragile hold on control, saw her brow pleat when it became difficult.

"I'm through crying," she said in a breathless voice.

He could see that she wanted to be, but she wasn't. Tears backed up in her eyes, puddled in her lower lids and spilled over.

He wrapped his arms around her and she sank slowly against him as she finally abandoned all efforts to remain in charge. Sobbing filled the sunny room, and Bobbi's tears dampened the neck and shoulder of Sin's flannel shirt.

"Crying is stupid," she complained as she continued to do just that.

He rubbed her back and rocked her gently from side to side. "Crying's part of being pregnant. It's in the book. You're supposed to be irritable, irrational and weepy."

"I am not irrational."

"Of course not."

She drew back to look at him, her face blotchy and swollen. "I'm not."

He cleared a tear away with his thumb. "I just agreed that you're not."

"You were patronizing me."

"I was thinking that you're normally irrational," he corrected gently, holding her loosely in the circle of his arms, "and it would be hard to tell if you were behaving that way as a result of erratic hormones or because you were just being yourself."

It occurred to her to push him away and stomp off to her workshop. But she discarded that option, and leaned back against him. She was sometimes irrational and she was certainly weepy. And she'd certainly prove irritability if she stormed away. So she simply settled back into the warm comfort of his arms and enjoyed the delicious sensation as they tightened around her.

"Does your book say when I'll get over this?"

"Soon. You'll experience fewer mood swings in your fifth month." He kissed the top of her head. "But you'll continue to be absentminded."

She frowned against his shirt, too comfortable to move. "I haven't been absentminded."

"I imagine all the details are different for every pregnancy." He lay back and brought her with him, pulling the other side of the bedspread over them.

She remained curled against him and asked without concern, "What are we doing?"

"We're going to take a nap," he replied.

"What about the puppy?"

"I brought her inside and closed her in the kitchen. She's fine." He turned slightly to settle Bobbi in the crook of his arm and readjust the bedspread.

"I should be working," she protested halfheartedly. "I should—"

He gave her a quick kiss that silenced her protest. "You should be resting. You haven't been sleeping very well. I've heard you tossing and turning."

"That's the way I sleep. Always has been."

"I don't remember that."

She nuzzled into him and felt herself begin to drift off. "You can't...judge by one night."

He was hoping not to have to. "Then you'll have to expand my data base."

But she was already asleep.

Chapter Seven

October

"I'm finished!" Bobbi exclaimed excitedly, hooking her arm in his and pulling him away from the vegetables he was chopping. "Come and see."

"Finished what?" he asked, tossing the half a carrot he still held at the chopping block as she dragged him toward her workshop. Buttercup bounded after them.

"The settee. Now, all we have to do is find a customer for it."

"We have one," he said.

She looked up at him in surprise as she pushed the door open. "We do? Who?"

"Gina wants it for a wedding present for a couple of kids that work at the inn."

"Oh." She smiled, pleased. "That's wonderful."

On a plastic tarp in the middle of the floor stood the finished piece, as elegant, he guessed, as the day some craftsman from the previous century put the finishing touches on it.

He walked around it in respectful silence. He wasn't an antique hunter himself, but he'd had enough of them forced on him by his mother to know a good restoration when he saw it.

She'd done a flawless job. The original wood now gleamed with life, and the tapestry fabric she'd chosen lent it a warmth and elegance that made him think the man who'd built it would be pleased with it.

"It's beautiful," he said finally. "No wonder you're sought after." He turned to grin at her. "But that didn't keep you busy very long."

She lifted a shoulder under his old sweater. "I have to learn to work faster and be more productive."

Silence followed her remark. He chose not to dispute it. In the two weeks they'd spent at the cabin, they'd found a companionable coexistence. He was determined that it would be more than that, but he was willing to bide his time.

She often made remarks intended, he was sure, to remind him that this was all just temporary. He ignored them.

"So, it's time to go garage-saleing," he observed.

"Right. Buttercup, no!" Bobbi made a grab for the puppy who'd found a loop of cane. She snatched it off a bottom shelf of the workbench and was running off with it.

Sin ran to block the doorway. Buttercup turned on a dime to run off in the other direction, head held high to avoid tripping on the loop. Her ears flapped as she ran and her eyes gleamed with the excitement of the new game.

Bobbi spread her arms wide and chased the puppy back to Sin. They trapped her between them, both laughing, and landed in a tangle on the braided mat in front of the door.

Barking excitedly, the cane abandoned for live prey, Buttercup leapt on top of them. Sin turned Bobbi into him protectively and felt and heard her laughter in his ear. His other ear had become a chew toy for Buttercup.

"How long before we can take her to obedience classes?" Bobbi asked, giggling and breathless.

"She has to be between six and eight months old to be mature enough to get the message." He pushed the jumping puppy aside and said firmly, "Buttercup, sit!"

Buttercup wagged her tail and continued to stand, watching him expectantly. He rolled his eyes.

"I thought you had a way with difficult females," Bobbi teased.

Fueled by an evil little spirit that had taken up residence on her shoulder, she was ever polite and cooperative, but she aimed every subtle, playful little barb she could his way.

It annoyed her that he was so complacently controlled in every aspect of their togetherness when the strain of always being within his reach was beginning to get to her.

It made no sense. She knew he was the wrong man.

So, why did she feel this pull toward him? Why didn't the knowledge that they could have nothing permanent together kill the desire that grew with each passing day?

Sin leaned over her on his elbow, his blue eyes dark and lazy. "Are you suggesting that was an idle boast?"

She saw the danger immediately—even realized that she'd invited it. While she considered the foolhardiness of accepting the challenge, or the safety of a quick retreat, he took the choice from her.

His mouth came down with possessive, even aggressive force. One hand cupped behind her head protected it from the cold concrete floor while the other traced a bold line down her body—over a full breast, over her ribs, over the swell where her flat tummy had been, along her thigh.

Her senses overloaded, unable to decide whether to concentrate on his hand or his mouth. A trembling path under her skin followed in the wake of his hand, turning every little nerve ending into a fluttering, protesting entity demanding another touch, another stroke.

But his kiss was making her toes curl, her knee hitch up in self-defense as a flutter of need rippled up the center of her.

She held on to his shoulders and let all her feelings free.

Sin felt the unknotting of her control and had to keep a firm grip on his. Her fingers wound in his hair, tickled his ears, raised gooseflesh on his scalp.

Bobbi strained closer to him, her plump breasts flattening against his chest, their predictable tips hardening from the contact. He pulled her even closer and traced a hand down her spine to catch a rounded hip in his palm and press her to him.

His body reacted strongly to the stimulus of hers and he took her little gasp into his mouth.

Then she pushed against him and he reluctantly allowed her to put a few inches between them.

"What are we doing?" she whispered in genuine concern.

He frowned. "Certainly it's familiar? We've done it before."

She pushed another inch's distance away. "No, I mean what are we *doing?*"

"You know very well what we're doing," he replied with mild impatience. "You started it."

That was true. He'd never held her a moment longer than she'd wanted him to.

"Well, I'm finishing it." She tried to break out of his hold and stand. Buttercup, interested in all the strange goings-on, wandered around and around them, whining.

Sin held fast, his expression altering subtly from that of tolerant understanding to one of guarded control.

"You know," he said quietly, "you keep acting as though your opinion is all that matters in this. There are two of us involved here."

"Three of us," she corrected judiciously.

"I'm not talking about the pregnancy. I'm talking about the relationship."

"The relationship," she put in calmly, "is about the pregnancy."

He studied her in surprise for a moment. Then he shook his head slowly, suddenly understanding something that had confused him until now. "No, it's not. Is that really what you thought?"

She looked into his eyes, trying to read there whether or not he spoke the truth. But becoming ensnared in his gaze was never safe for her. It made her want what she couldn't have, made her willing to risk what she shouldn't. She lowered her eyes to his shirtfront.

"If you'd had any interest in me other than this baby," she said sternly, "you'd have called."

"I was waiting for you to call me."

Bobbi raised her eyes to his at that, annoyance negating the danger. "You egotist! Despite the changes in courtship rules, the gentleman usually still takes the lead. Only in our case, the relationship didn't include a gentleman."

He took the insult in good humor. "How do you think you got invited to Rebecca's party?" he asked.

She studied him doubtfully. "What do you mean?"

"She showed me the piece, and told me about the pretty blonde who restored it for her. Seems Wyatt Raleigh put her on to you."

Bobbi's eyes widened. "Gina's father?"

"Right. I put two and two together and suggested she invite you to the party."

She frowned, feeling vaguely disappointed. "I thought she invited me because she was pleased with my work."

"She did," he assured her. "What she wanted to do in the beginning was invite you to a private dinner at her home, just her and Ridley and you..." He grinned. "And me to make up the numbers. She's been trying to match me up for years. But I thought you might refuse a private invitation, particularly if you knew I was involved, so I suggested she invite you to the party and not mention me at all. I asked her to pretend she didn't even know we knew each other.''

Bobbi continued to eye him suspiciously. "You're telling me you *wanted* to see me again."

"Yes."

"As long as you didn't have to call me and let me know how you felt."

The statement implied censure and he was perfectly willing to accept it.

He sighed and sat up, pulling her with him. Buttercup, thinking action was imminent, barked in their faces.

"Down!" Sin shouted. "Sit!"

Buttercup did both, surprising them.

Sin turned back to Bobbi as though he'd fully expected the puppy's obedience. "The embarrassing truth is," he said with a self-deprecating smile, "I'm vulnerable to rejection. As a child I was repeatedly pushed aside by my parents while they globe-trotted for my father's work. I grew up determined no one would ever make me feel that way again."

Touched by his admission, but still afraid to give too much, Bobbi said gently, "Everyone's afraid of rejection."

He nodded. "I know. But it still is hard to swallow—especially when I made love with a woman who then walked away the next morning as though it had been nothing."

"I didn't know where I was," Bobbi defended herself quickly. "Not physically, although that was confusing for the first few minutes after I opened my eyes. But I didn't know where I was emotionally. I mean, it wasn't like I did that sort of thing all the time. And you're rich."

He closed his eyes and shook his head. "You keep saying that like it's a social disease. Being rich is fun. I like it. You'd like it, too."

"I live a simple life, Sin."

"So do I, Bobbi. It just has more money in it."

She sighed and squared her shoulders. "We're getting away from the issue." She winced, then smiled thinly. "What was it? I've forgotten."

He laughed and hugged her close. "So have I. I think the point is that it doesn't matter. We're together because we're doing one of the most wonderful jobs God ever hands out. I don't want us to clutter it up with restrictions. I want us to enjoy it."

"But we have to consider," she pointed out insistently, "what happens when it's over."

"It won't be *over*," he said. "It'll be just beginning—a new life that *we* made."

"But you didn't really *want* to make it."

"Did you?"

She stared at him. It was a point well taken.

"That's not the issue," he went on earnestly. "But the reality of a baby coming changes everything. It's a wonder, a miracle."

"I know that. But it's a miracle with far-reaching ramifications."

"That's right. So far-reaching that we should give ourselves time to consider and examine all of them. We have to get to know each other if we're going to understand our baby."

Bobbi stared at him helplessly. This was all so far from what she'd planned when she'd discovered she was pregnant. She'd determined to do it alone, to love and raise this baby with everything spiritual and physical she had. She'd been prepared to do it without the baby's father—even thought she'd prefer it that way.

And here he was talking about love and understanding and beginnings, sounding as though he already loved it as much as she did.

Sin saw her weakening. He was enough of a lawyer to know when to stop pressing his advantage and let his witness win the case for him.

"Tell you what," he said. "Let's just go garage-saleing and talk about this when you're feeling more up to it."

She gave him a look that told him she knew what he was doing, but she was going to let him do it anyway.

He got to his feet and pulled her up with him. Buttercup began prancing around them.

"You don't go garage-saleing in the middle of the afternoon," she said, dusting off the seat of her sweats.

He ruffled the dog's ears as it jumped up against him, then pushed it down with a gently spoken command. "Why not?" he asked.

She opened the door to the kitchen and Sin and Buttercup followed her inside. "Because all the best stuff will be gone. You go early in the morning on the first day of the sale."

"Ah," he said, "I didn't realize it was a science." He took a dog treat from a canister on the counter and tossed it to Buttercup, who settled down under the kitchen table to munch it earnestly.

"There's a flea market at the Presbyterian Church that starts tomorrow," she said. "Want some juice?"

"Please." He sat at the table and watched her pour jewel-bright orange juice into two glasses. Buttercup had moved onto his foot to enjoy her treat and he found himself affected by this pleasantly domestic situation.

"It was in the paper last night." She handed him a glass and sat across from him. "Starts at eight in the morning. Want to go?"

"Sure."

"I'll fix dinner tonight so you can rest up."

"Rest up?" He raised a wary eyebrow. "This is like a triathlon, or something?"

"Close. We'll see how much stamina you really have."

His eyebrow rose higher and with suggestive accent. "I thought we already tested that."

She fought the blush courageously, but lost. She brushed her bangs aside and cleared her throat as memories of that night rose to deepen her color. In light of what his nearness did to her these days, she found herself in serious confusion.

Sin found something charmingly artless in a blush on a pregnant woman. He stood and snapped his fingers at the puppy.

"If we have to be in fighting trim for this, we'd better train by taking Buttercup for a walk."

She groaned. "I shop on a regular basis. I don't need to train."

"You don't give birth on a regular basis, though. You've got to get in shape for that."

"Sin..."

"Come on, don't argue." He tugged on her arm until she was on her feet. "The doctor said you need light exercise. I've got something special planned for lunch and you'll appreciate it more if you've worked up an appetite."

"What?" she asked, distracted enough to let him lead her and the jumping dog to the French doors.

"Lasagna," he said.

She stopped dead, staring at him in smiling wonder. "You're kidding!"

He pulled her gently through the open door and slid it closed behind her.

"No, I'm not. It's vegetable lasagna, but I defy you to tell the difference."

"And I can really have it? You won't snatch it away from me at the last moment like some kind of test of my character, or something?"

"Of course not. You can even have seconds if you really like it."

"Topped with Parmesan?"

"Freshly grated."

"Garlic toast?"

"That might be pushing it. I'll put a few croutons on your salad."

"I'll get my jacket."

SIN AWOKE to Bobbi straddling his body. For a moment, he thought he was still dreaming. Lately his subconscious had been toying with him at night, taking all the fantasies he now lived with on a daily basis and making him experience them on the high-graphics monitor of his mind.

He relaxed into his pillow, happy to let her have her way with him. He imagined how it had happened. She'd been longing for him every bit as much as he'd been longing for her. She'd awoken in the night, desperate for him—her body aching as his ached, and yearning to bridge the gap between them.

She'd come naked to his bed, and he could feel the silk of her skin under his hands as they traced the warm, supple line of her thighs, over the curve of her hip, along her sides and over her breasts.

She was saying his name urgently over and over, the beautiful repetition broken occasionally by a puffy sigh and the stroke of her hand along his cheek.

Her knees felt like a delicious vise squeezing his hips, the weight of her resting on his groin and doing a sinuous little wriggle that...

"Sinclair! Come on!"

He came to the brink of awareness with the realization that he was being throttled. The sweet voice of his dreams was now raised in his ear and sharply demanding. The fingers running along his cheek now applied a little slap there.

Sin surfaced from his wonderful fantasy and opened his eyes to find that his subconscious had honestly transmitted events but his own frustrated desire had put the wrong definition on them.

"Thank God!" Bobbi exclaimed. "I was beginning to think you'd lapsed into a coma. Are you always this hard to wake up?"

She *was* straddling his waist, but she wasn't naked. She was wearing a pair of stone-colored pants and a bright red T-shirt. She wore a bandanna around her neck cowboy style. She'd done something to her hair that gave it a little curl, and he found himself staring at it, liking the way it softened the contours of her face. She had makeup on and a sparkle in her bright eyes.

Her soft, rounded bottom was still resting on his groin, however, and made it very difficult for him to abandon the fantasy altogether.

He put his hands to her thighs and let himself believe she'd awakened him for romantic reasons rather than for whatever she had in mind.

"I assure you I am not comatose," he said. "Want to come to bed?"

The hand that in his dream had stroked his cheek gave it a gentle cuff. "I want you *out* of bed."

He smiled and placed her a little more carefully. "Want to make love in the shower?"

"In your dreams."

She was right about that.

"I want you to come and have breakfast."

He got a whiff of coffee and . . . cinnamon?

"You cooked?" he asked in disbelief.

In the two and a half weeks they'd been in the cabin, she'd made coffee several times, but her idea of preparing lunch had been crackers and cheese and a can of soup.

"Sort of." She braced both hands on his chest to lever herself off his waist.

He grasped her arms to help her, feeling naked and deprived when her weight was gone from him.

"What time is it?" he asked, rolling his head to look at the clock. It was just after six.

"I know it's early," she said, bustling around the room, taking the jeans he'd left on a chair near the bed and tossing them at his blanketed form. "But the bazaar starts at eight, and if we want to be there at opening you've got to get moving."

"It's only a ten minute drive, Bobbi," he said, dragging himself onto his elbows.

She was looking through the things in his closet, and pulled out a blue-and-gray flannel shirt.

"That's old," he told her.

"Is it?" She studied it a moment, then tossed it at him, too. "I like you in it," she admitted, seeming to surprise herself, then she resumed a brisk manner and started opening drawers. "Where are your socks?"

He turned on his side and leaned on an elbow, watching her. "I like to dress myself," he said, then grinned when she looked at him over her shoulder. "Unless, of course, you'd actually like to put them on me."

She turned back to the dresser, found the right drawer, withdrew a folded pair of athletic socks and came to sit on the edge of the bed beside him.

She was close enough that he could smell her fragrance and see a glint of humor in her eyes.

"Let me put it to you this way." She held up the pear-shaped folded socks. "You can put these socks on yourself, or..." She folded a fist and waggled it under his nose. "Or I could actually put some of these 'socks' on you. Now, which is it going to be?"

Bobbi didn't know why she was still in the room. Well, she did, but it was difficult to admit to it.

She should have tossed the socks at him and prompted him to hurry. Instead she was letting herself be drawn into the tension crackling from him. It had her now, and held her immobile while Sin's deceptively lazy eyes went from the socks in her hand to her face.

"Big talk," he said, "for a couch potato who can't even button her jeans anymore."

"I have the muscle to back up the threat," she assured him lightly, waggling the fist again. Everything inside her was quickening. "I can't button my jeans because the challenge I present you is *two* against one. You're sure you want to take us on?"

"I do my best work on cases everyone's sure I can't win."

"I'm not talking about a sissy mental exercise," she said. She was taking this too far, but she couldn't seem to stop. She was having too much fun—and she had to see how it all...

She was on her back in the middle of the bed almost before she knew what happened. She heard her own laughter as he pressed her into the pillows.

"Think it's funny, do you?" he asked silkily, holding her still with the weight of his upper body across hers. "A man devotes himself to restoring a woman to some semblance of physical fitness and she gets a little cocky and tries to use it against him. I think someone needs a lesson in humility."

She rolled her eyes and made a scornful sound while still laughing. "Like *you* could teach anyone anything about humility. Could we please have breakfast?"

"Not until you learn that threats are not acceptable negotiating tactics."

"Sinclair, you kidnapped me," she pointed out. She heard herself say the words and realized in some surprise that she truly no longer thought of it that way. He'd spoiled and cosseted her the past few weeks and, at this moment, she wouldn't want to be anywhere else.

As that thought flowed over her and into her to become part of her reality, she stared into his eyes and felt just a little helpless.

She saw his eyes note and puzzle over her sudden seriousness, and made herself get it together. "You kidnapped me," she repeated in a jocular tone. "Is that acceptable negotiating tactics?"

"I'll show you what's acceptable," he said. His arms burrowed under her and crossed around her as his mouth closed over hers. His lips drove her mad, pressing her into the pillows, drowning her in goose down and wild sensation.

Her shirt was suddenly over her face and she was trapped in it while his lips dotted kisses across her waist at the band of her pants. Then his fingertips delved into the fabric and pulled it down to her hipbones.

"Sin!" she tried to complain, but was trapped in her blouse and by the weight of his body.

"Hush," he scolded gently. "I'm communing with my child." He planted kisses all around the little mound of her stomach.

Everything inside Bobbi shuddered, sensitized to his touch, taunting her with little tremors and the demand that she abandon all caution and constraint and let him love her as he had nearly five months ago.

Then, in the midst of all her own physical responses, she felt the baby move. She'd thought she'd been feeling it for the past few weeks, but the movement was so light, so delicate, similar to the bursting of a bubble or the flutter of a wing.

Then Sin was leaning over her. He pulled her shirt down and looked into her face, ever sensitive to her every change of mood or expression.

"What?" he demanded.

"The baby kicked," she said, taking his hand and placing it on her stomach. "Can you feel it?" she asked excitedly.

They stared at each other, eyes wide with wonder, waiting for another movement.

His hand on Bobbi's stomach, his eyes locked with hers, Sin felt something in his life shift and change—something he'd lost and something he'd gained.

He'd loved a woman and made a child. That fact would ripple down the years into a future he wouldn't see but had affected. It boggled his mind.

"Rats," Bobbi said with genuine disappointment when the baby continued to be quiet. "It's such a small sensation, you probably wouldn't have felt it anyway. Next time."

"Next time." He leaned down to kiss her gently, tenderly, with all the indescribable pride and possession he felt in her—his woman, mother of his child.

He scooped her out of bed, put her on her feet and sent her toward the kitchen with a playful swat.

He stood under the hot shower and set the spray for full force. A few moments before he'd watched something change in her eyes. She'd gone from tolerant houseguest to willing, even happy cohabitant. And just a moment ago, she'd tried to share with him the delight of feeling the baby move—and she'd been disappointed when he hadn't.

He was making progress.

Chapter Eight

Sin wouldn't have believed it if he hadn't seen it for himself. Walking Buttercup around and around the church parking lot packed with booths and tables festively draped with crepe paper and banners, he kept his eye on Bobbi, who'd certainly proven to know her flea markets.

Several other die-hard treasure seekers had also appeared fifteen minutes early to be there when the chain-link barrier was dropped and the market officially opened.

Bobbi held her own against a pair of middle-aged women in elegant suits whom he guessed to be partners in an antique business, and a very short older woman with a shopping bag over her arm that she used like a battering ram. Like an army on the move, the four women checked out every table.

Bobbi was the only one who lingered at a roped off section in the back of the lot packed with furniture. After a cursory tour through, the other women left her alone to pick her way through the clutter and examine in detail every item that interested her.

When Sin saw her lean dangerously far over a chair to study the back of a love seat behind it, he put Buttercup in the Blazer and loped back to Bobbi.

"What are you trying to do?" he asked, lifting her from the small space between a dresser and the chair where she'd gotten stuck.

"I want to see the bottom of that table," she said, grinning sheepishly at him. "I forget I'm not very agile anymore."

He lifted the chair out of her way, and finding no place to put it safely, continued to hold it.

She got down on her knees and exclaimed excitedly, "Possum belly bins!" He looked around in concern, grateful no one seemed to be watching.

"What?" he asked softly, flatly.

"Possum belly bins." She opened one to show him the deep, curved bottom. "It's an old baker's table. These bins once contained flour and meal."

"Is that good?" he asked.

"It's a present from heaven at two hundred dollars!" Her eyes lost the glow of discovery for a moment, and she said practically, "We never talked about how much of a budget I have for this kind of thing."

"Tell me I can put the chair down," he said, "and I give you carte blanche to get whatever you want."

"That isn't practical."

"I've never been practical."

"You have to put a limit on me or you'll find yourself in debtors' prison before the baby's born."

"If you start shopping at Sotheby's, we'll consider a limit, but for right now get whatever you like."

She looked like a little girl given free rein in a doll shop. "Really?"

"Really."

"Thank you!" She hugged him fiercely and he had to quickly shift the chair to one hand to save her nose from the sharp edge of a rocker. He set the chair down behind her, prepared to enjoy the embrace, but she was already a few yards ahead of him, beckoning him to follow. "There's an old steamer trunk back here that's more interesting than valuable, but it might be fun in..."

She carried on as he picked his way through the jumble of junky furniture.

He was exhausted by lunchtime and had taken Buttercup for a second tour of the grounds when she came toward him with both hands full of what appeared to be steaming white paper.

"Lunch," she announced proudly, leading the way to the grouping of furniture against the church wall. The largest piece, the settee, had been tagged with a hastily penciled Sinclair.

She sat on the settee and scooted into the corner. He took that as an invitation to sit beside her. Buttercup stood with her forepaws in his lap, whining and sniffing the contents of Bobbi's hands. Hot dogs.

"Down!" Sin ordered.

The puppy complied, but without loss of enthusiasm. She sat at his feet, tail swishing, whining pathetically. She licked her chops and never took her eyes off the food.

Bobbi held the three hot dogs out to Sin. He put one in its paper on the ground for Buttercup, then took one for himself.

"You know what's in this?" he asked, frowning over it in mild disapproval.

She took a big bite of hers and nodded. She chewed and swallowed. "Memories of Girl Scout camp outs, county fairs, the food concession at the beach when I was a little girl. It contains the virtual *soul* of baseball, the..."

"Stop!" He shook his head and grinned at her as she delved into the shopping bag she slipped from her shoulder and handed him a can of Pepsi. "Enjoy your hot dog. Far be it from me to upset your childhood memories or the American spirit of baseball. Thank you. What's in the bag?"

She took another bite of hot dog and produced several old pieces of needlework, a sack of ribbon and trim odds and ends, an empty picture frame, a doll-size quilt and a large plastic pumpkin that probably came to the bazaar via a dime store twenty years before.

At his skeptical look she explained, "It'll be Halloween before you know it."

"We could probably have bought a *new* plastic pumpkin for whatever you paid for that 'antique.'"

"Wrong. I got it out of the dime box. We have to pick weeds for it."

"Weeds?"

"Yeah, you know. The stuff on the side of the road. What do they have around here? Thistle? Gypsy grass?"

He popped the last bite of hot dog into his mouth and shook his head as he chewed. "Don't know," he said finally. "I don't usually go grubbing on the side of the road when I come here. But, we'll check it out. Whatever makes you happy. Ready to go?"

She gave him a sunny smile and asked hopefully, "Can I do one more tour to make sure I haven't missed anything?"

He groaned and glanced at his watch. "Ten minutes. You've been hard at it for almost four hours. You need to put your feet up for a while."

"I'm fine," she insisted.

"Ten minutes," he repeated. "Go ahead. I'll get rid of the trash and put Buttercup in the Blazer."

He was walking back toward Bobbi across the lot now crowded with shoppers and children. The smell of hot dogs and popcorn competed with the freshness of fall in the air and he took a deep breath, letting himself enjoy the simple pleasure of the warm scene reminiscent of a primitive print.

Colorful banners flew in the midday breeze, people in bright sweaters and buffalo-plaid jackets wandered through the rows of old merchandise looking for treasure, and the black cat that apparently lived on the property bordering the church watched it all from a snoozing position on the narrow top rail of the fence that separated them.

An old oak at the end of the lot was just beginning to turn color, and a leaf sailed down as he watched.

This was life in slow-motion, something he seldom had the opportunity to enjoy.

He caught sight of Bobbi, pushing her way through the crowd at a booth selling candy. She waved at him as she emerged, laughing and clutching a white sack to her.

Still too far apart for conversation, he shook his head at her latest purchase, trying to look stern but succeeding only, he was sure, in looking indulgent. She was laughingly impenitent.

He noticed the old man because the two pieces he carried, one under each arm, seemed too heavy for the slightness of his stooped frame. He was coming from a truck parked at the curb, and about to converge with Sin and Bobbi at the edge of the lot.

Under one arm was a fussy maple curio cabinet, and under the other, an old, scarred cradle.

Sin and Bobbi spotted the cradle at the same moment, then looked up into each other's eyes in silent communication.

"'Lo," the man said with a polite nod as he angled sideways to walk around them.

"Hello," Sin said, going toward him to take the curio cabinet. "Let me help you with that."

The old man expelled a breath of relief. "Thank you. Little arthritic this morning. How're things going?" He looked around at the milling crowd. "Was afraid I'd be too late with my donations. Don't look like it, though."

Bobbi was running a hand over the cradle's hood. "You brought the cradle to sell?" she asked.

He nodded, sharp blue eyes behind wire-rimmed glasses softening as they noted Bobbi's pregnancy. "Yeah. I see you're in the market for one."

Bobbi glanced at Sin, her eyes telling him they'd happened on something very special.

"This is very Early American, isn't it?" she asked the old man, her voice filled with the awe she felt. "Pine sides. Oak ends and frame. Late eighteenth century."

She ran her fingers over an almost imperceptible notched pattern and felt the jolt she always experienced when she made contact with some unknown artist from another time.

The old man nodded matter-of-factly and groaned as he bent to place the large cradle on the ground. "One of my great-greats—I forget how many—was a ship's captain, and built it for his firstborn in Fairhaven, Massachusetts."

Bobbi sank to her knees, still touching the cradle's scarred hood.

"Came west with his granddaughter, my great-grandmother, who married a shopkeeper, and had a daughter somewhere on the Applegate Trail." He smiled and put both hands behind him and stretched his waist. "Since then it's traveled back to New York with my grandfather, who taught economics at Yale, then back here again with my father, a simple farmer like myself. It's a well-traveled piece."

Sin noted the gold wedding band he wore, thin with age, but was reluctant to ask the obvious question. Bobbi, however, did it with diplomacy.

"Shouldn't it stay in your family?" Her expression had changed subtly from covetousness to protectiveness.

"No more Coopers to pass it to," he said with a philosophical sigh. Bobbi thought she detected pain there, under the surface of acceptance. "I was an only child, and Janie and I lost our son in Vietnam. Was all we had."

"I'm sorry," Sin said quietly. The mood of the folksy, fall day had suddenly changed to remind him that time and everything it moved along was fleeting, and that fate often had little sense of continuity.

Bobbi couldn't speak.

The old man looked from one to the other. "Janie never did want to give it up. Been wanting to put it in the church sale for years, but couldn't talk her into it." He hesitated, his forehead wrinkled and he coughed. "Janie passed away in the spring. Smartest woman God ever made, but she was wrong about this cradle. There've been lots of babies loved in it. It should have another one in it. Maybe you'd like to give it a new start?" he speculated with a paternal tilt of his head down at Bobbi. "Send it down another string of generations until the rockers are worn right off it."

Sin looked down at Bobbi for confirmation that she wanted it, but she wouldn't look up at him. She just pushed the cradle with her fingertips, watching it rock from side to side.

He'd come to understand her emotional moods, could even see them coming despite the suddenness of their changes. But he knew he couldn't put this reaction down to rioting hormones. He could guess what she was thinking—that they'd be assuming responsibility for this legendary cradle under false pretenses. They were not the beginning of a dynasty. They were the result of a moonlit night and a mutual need.

He was going to fix that.

"Mr. Cooper," he asked, getting a better grip on the increasingly heavy curio cabinet. "Where were you heading with the cabinet and the cradle? To the ladies' auxiliary that's handling the furniture?"

"Yes." Mr. Cooper laughed apologetically and tried to take back the cabinet. "I'm sorry! Got so involved in my story, I forgot you were holding that."

"I'll take it over," Sin said, "then maybe you and the ladies can decide on a price while my...while Bobbi and I talk it over."

"You bet."

Cooper followed him to the pair of middle-aged ladies who'd sold them most of the things they'd put aside. He introduced him, then sent him back to Bobbi while the three huddled over a price.

Bobbi was now on her feet, arms folded, looking down at the cradle. Three other people, a man and two women, were now clustered around the cradle in the grass. Sin took them for newlyweds and a mother-in-law.

"I *have* to have it," the young woman was saying emphatically to the man. "Jason, buy it for me, please." The last word was for effect. There was command, not pleading, in the voice.

"It's bound to be expensive, Megan," Jason replied. "The lady here—" he pointed upward at Bobbi "—says it's colonial. That's an antique, Meggie, not a secondhand cradle. Besides, that lady has a prior claim on it."

"She said she was undecided," Megan corrected. "If we decide before she does, it's ours. I want it."

The older woman wrinkled her lip at it. "It won't go with the white provincial baby furniture I've already bought you."

"It's an antique, Mother," Megan said. "Shelly Jansen's house is filled with antiques. I don't have *one.*"

Her mother frowned. "You have Grandmother Billings's armoire."

Megan huffed. "That isn't an antique, it's a hand-me-down."

"I'm sorry." Sin lifted the cradle from the midst of the arguing trio and gave them a charming smile. "We have prior claim to the cradle."

Megan cast a glare at Bobbi. "She said she was undecided."

He gave Bobbi a challenging smile. "She forgets, sometimes, that she isn't in this alone. I *am* decided. Excuse us." He tucked the cradle under one arm and put the other around Bobbi, drawing her toward Mr. Cooper and the ladies of the auxiliary.

"We don't deserve it," Bobbi said moodily.

"You'd prefer it went to Megan the Monster so she can have an antique because Sherry's house is full of them?"

"Shelly's house," Bobbi corrected. "And you don't understand."

"Yes, I do. Every time the subject comes up, I know what you're going to say before you say it. 'It'll never work,' he quoted in a bored tone. 'You're the wrong man, Sinclair, and you're a playboy who can walk away when the mood strikes him.'" They settled into line behind a couple paying for an old mangle, and he squeezed her shoulder. "Tell me I'm wrong."

"You're impossible," she grumbled.

"True," he said amiably. "But that's not the same thing."

Bobbi held the cradle in her lap on the drive home, afraid Buttercup might consider it appropriate for teething if placed in the back with her.

Pieces from the past always gave her a feeling of connection, a link with the people who'd lived with and used them. When she didn't know the piece's history, she sometimes made one up for her own entertainment, based on what it made her feel.

But she knew all about the cradle. It had rocked babies for six or seven generations, until an untimely death had cut its work short. It shook her to touch the pockmarked wood and know that flailing little fists from two hundred years ago had touched it, too.

It had traveled back and forth across the country several times and was now going home with her and Sin to an uncertain future.

"If you don't quit moping," Sin threatened as he pulled into the driveway, "I'll give you steamed vegetables for dinner."

"I'm not moping," she denied with a frown at him. "I'm thinking about all the little lives the cradle has launched and wondering..." She hesitated, finding what she felt difficult to express, even to understand.

"You're wondering if we're qualified to take up the torch." Sin braked to a stop and turned off the engine. They looked at each other in silence.

"I hate it when you do that," she said.

He looked around them in confusion. "Do what? Stop the car? Driving through the garage door isn't good for it. Doesn't do much for the car, either."

She knew *he* knew what she meant. "When you try to put all the complicated things I feel into one clever, pithy sentence that's supposed to sum it all up."

He opened his door and Buttercup immediately snaked between the front seats to follow him out. He came around the hood to open Bobbi's door and take the cradle from her.

"What you feel is very simple," he said, putting the cradle under one arm to help her down with the other hand. "The reasons you give yourself for denying that it's true are what're complicated."

"Oh, really." She reached in for her shopping bag and they headed for the front door, the dog leaping around them. She leaned against the door frame while he unlocked the door. "And how can you presume to know what I feel?"

He pushed the door open and smiled down into her upturned face. He looked her over slowly, feature by feature, then concentrated on her eyes.

"Because it's all right there," he said softly. "In the heart of your cat's eyes. You pretend to be aloof, just like a worldly cat, but tempt you with a warm fire and a welcoming lap to sit in and you're putty. There's no shame in needing someone, you know."

He was right, but she didn't want to consider that. And she resented him for pointing it out. "What..." she demanded, walking past him with her chin up, just like the cat to which he'd compared her, "does that have to do with the Cooper cradle?"

She tossed her bag onto the sofa, sank beside it and kicked off her shoes.

Sin put the cradle on the carpet in front of her and went into the kitchen. Buttercup sprawled in front of the fireplace.

"It's all part of your self-protective process," Sin called out. She heard the refrigerator door open and the sound of liquid being poured. "You like it here, but you keep telling yourself you can't stay here, you know the best thing for our baby..." He emerged from the kitchen, a tall glass in each hand "...would be for us to get married and give it a real family." He sat beside her, handed her one of the glasses of juice and added with a very level look into her eyes, "And you're falling in love with me, but you keep fighting it. You're so afraid that the man who didn't call you could make you happy after all."

She turned and met his even gaze. "What woman in her right mind would want to be married to a man who required that she always make the first emotional move?"

"I did that only once," he replied, looking away from her to frown into his glass. Then he turned back and shrugged a shoulder apologetically. "I have my own vulnerabilities. I explained that."

He reached out with his foot and gave the cradle a little nudge that started it rocking. "And this is no longer the Cooper cradle. It's the Sinclair cradle. And we can give it the future Mr. Cooper thought it should have if you'll loosen up and share with me."

They stared at each other, she fighting the pull in his direction, he reaching a hand along the back of the sofa to cup her cheek, making it difficult for her to draw back.

"You know you want to," he whispered.

"I can't just do what I want to do," she replied, her voice tinged with uncertainty. He put his glass on the coffee table, took hers from her and placed it beside his. "I have to think for two now."

"Why don't you just let me think for three?"

"Because it isn't safe." Even as she said the words, she rubbed her cheek against his palm. "You'd just do what you want."

"But, what I want is for you and the baby to be safe and comfortable and happy. Isn't that what you want?" His fingertips reached into the short hair at the back of her neck where she always grew tense when she fretted about the baby. He began to rub in small, gentle circles.

She expelled a soft sigh and closed her eyes. "Yes, of course. Under... under the right circumstances."

"Come here." He turned her so that her back was to him and she was tucked up against his bent leg. Applying both hands, he loosened the muscles at her shoulders. When her head began to loll, he asked, "What do you consider the right circumstances?"

It was becoming difficult to think. Her body seemed to be turning to liquid and her brain to mush. All she was aware of were his hands and their strong, circular, somehow seductive movements across her back and along her spine.

"Maybe..." she said slowly, because everything about her seemed to be slowing down. "Maybe if you struggled from paycheck to... paycheck..."

"I wouldn't be able to give the baby everything you'd probably like it to have. Now I can see that it has those things."

She stiffened a little under his hands. "*Things* aren't everything."

"Of course they aren't," he replied calmly. "That's why I want to give you love and security as well. That's why I want to marry you."

He heard her sharp intake of breath, felt the little shudder of feeling that ran up her spine. She turned slowly to look into his eyes. Hers were wide and stunned.

"What?"

"I want to marry you," he repeated.

As she continued to stare at him, he laughed softly. "Why are you so surprised?"

"I suppose," she said softly, still staring into his eyes as though there were a crawl line there she could read, "a lawyer likes to see everything under contract."

"A man," he corrected slowly, soberly, "is possessive about what belongs to him."

"You want to own me and the baby." It was a statement that hinted of accusation.

He studied her a moment before answering, his expression quietly confident. "I do already," he said, putting his arms loosely around her. "I want to love you and care for you...." He placed a large hand gently over her abdomen. "And I want the two of you to love me."

And it was at that moment, with Sin's body inclined toward Bobbi's, and hers cradled in his arm, that the baby reacted.

Bobbi started and Sin's eyes widened in surprise.

"Did you feel it?" she whispered excitedly, hitching closer and holding his hand firmly against her.

The second kick was almost as firm.

"God!" Sin felt his child against his palm, a tickle of sensation so quick he needed Bobbi's confirming nod to assure himself he hadn't imagined it. Then it was still.

"God!" he said again. He hugged her to him, filled with a reverence for his situation he hadn't experienced until this moment.

Bobbi felt the tenderness in him and it was her undoing. She'd been charmed by his kindness, alarmed by his possessiveness, wary of his sexiness and frankly afraid of his determination to make this relationship work out his way.

She hadn't known this real love was there, but she'd seen it in his eyes when the baby kicked. He'd been awed, delighted, touched—and she'd felt the strength of his emotion when he'd taken her in his arms.

She'd once thought all his feelings were for the baby, but she saw now that they weren't. It could be that the feelings he had for her were because the baby he loved was contained within her. But she didn't think so. Possibly the three of them were simply too entangled at that point in time to even exist without the other. They'd embarked on a course together that required the three of them for fruition.

Whatever the reason, Bobbi gave herself over to the love and warmth she felt wrapped in Sin's arms. This was what she'd lost and now she had it back.

Sin drew back and looked into Bobbi's eyes. His were dark with the love that surrounded them and a need she understood very well.

"I need to make love to you," he whispered.

She looped her arms around his neck and smiled. "Yes," she said. "You do."

Chapter Nine

Afternoon sun streamed into Sin's bedroom through two small-paned windows. It made a golden checkered pattern on a cedar chest at the foot of a pencil-post bed, and on an oak chest of drawers against the wall.

Bobbi felt its warmth as Sin placed her in the middle of the still-rumpled blankets. A colorful quilt had been thrown back on one side. She smiled as she remembered waking him that morning. Had it only been hours ago? It seemed as though a lot of things had changed since they'd encountered Mr. Cooper and his cradle.

"You didn't make your bed," she teased softly as Sin sat beside her and pulled a pillow under her head.

"You were rushing me, if you'll recall." He leaned over her, his eyes dark and wicked as he grinned. "Or maybe I had a premonition."

She cupped the back of his head and pulled him down to her. She didn't really care how she came to be here. The sheets smelled of his subtle cologne and his aggressive maleness. It was like a perfume that enfolded her and made her happy to be right where she was.

"Bobbi." He whispered her name before his mouth opened over hers. His tongue dipped inside and he drew deeply, showing her what he intended, inviting her to follow.

She needed little encouragement. She kissed him back, her tongue nudging and entwining with his, showing him that she wanted what he wanted, inviting him to proceed.

He drew away, bracing a hand on the pillow on either side of her head and smiling gently. "This is perfectly safe for you. I consulted my book."

She reached up to run the tip of her finger along his bottom lip. "When you had your premonition?"

"No. When I bought the book," he admitted with a small laugh at himself. Then he grew serious and his eyes seemed to devour her. "Making love to you again has been on my mind for months."

She dropped her hand and blinked in surprise. "But we hated each other during the Memorial Day weekend, and you saw me again only three weeks ago."

He inclined his head to indicate that didn't matter. "I know. But I've been thinking about you every night since *that* night. The wait for you has seemed interminable."

It shamed her a little to think that all those nights she'd lain awake after learning she was pregnant, she'd despised him for never giving her a second thought.

"I thought you didn't care," she said.

"What do you think now?"

She sighed and ran her hands lovingly down his face. "That we've wasted an awful lot of time. And we shouldn't waste another moment."

"Very astute." He turned his lips into her hand, then straightened and reached under her T-shirt to curl his fingers into the waistband of her slacks and panties.

Bobbi reached down to grasp the slacks' pleats and held on, preventing him from tugging them down.

"I'm going to look like a medicine ball," she warned.

Sin raised that eyebrow. It seemed to say he thought she was crazy. "You're supposed to get round," he said.

"I'm round enough, and I'm only four and a half months."

"Almost five," he corrected, "and you're being vain and silly."

"You haven't seen me," she insisted, holding fast to the fabric of her slacks as he tugged again.

"No, I haven't," he said, "and at this rate I'm not going to. I thought you said we've wasted enough time."

"I'll let go," she said, bargaining half playfully, "if you promise to close your eyes."

He rejected that suggestion quickly. "Absolutely not. But I have an idea." He leaned forward, took the scarf tied around her neck and raised it until it became a mask. "We'll close *your* eyes. Then you won't have to worry about how you look."

"Sin . . ." she tried to protest.

"Hush," he ordered softly, "or I'll put it over your mouth. Now, please. You and this baby are a gift to me. I want to enjoy unwrapping you."

Bobbi wondered if the words held more significance because she heard them without seeing them spoken. She wasn't distracted by the shape of his lips or the expression in his eyes. The words alone, spoken in his quiet rumbling voice, rolled over her. *"You and this baby are a gift to me. I want to enjoy unwrapping you."*

It was difficult to maintain self-consciousness or embarrassment when one was thought of as a present.

She felt his fingertips at her waist again and relaxed into the pillows as he tugged down her slacks and panties. She lifted up to help him clear them of her hips, then felt their slow removal down her thighs, over her knees and past her ankles. He disposed of them soundlessly.

She felt the gentle pinch of his fingers on her big toe, still clad in woolly socks. "Want to leave these on?" he asked.

"Please," she said. "My feet are always freezing."

"Right."

There was an instant's silence and she wondered a little nervously if finally seeing the plumping of her body had changed his mind about his gift. It was one thing to idealize a pregnant woman, but quite another to...

The analytical thought disintegrated when she felt his lips on her abdomen. His warm mouth kissed a path across the baby, the puff of his breath an erotic counterpoint to the reverence of his lips.

Then she felt his hands there, molded over the dome of her stomach, moving gently, exploratively, as though he were trying to feel the child inside.

The sightlessness the bandanna caused made her aware of every tiny movement he made. She swore she could feel his fingerprint against her as his hands moved up under her shirt.

She could almost feel the molecular structure of her own flesh as the stroke of his fingertips ran over it. Time was elongated, sensation magnified. One little touch stretched seconds into minutes, into hours.

She felt paradoxically relaxed and unbearably enervated. She wanted the gentle strokes to go on forever. And she wasn't sure she could bear another moment.

He gathered the hem of the T-shirt up and she raised her arms to allow its removal. He stopped before pulling the shirt over her head.

"If you're willing to be reasonable," he said, and she could hear the touch of humor in his voice, "I'll remove the bandanna."

She almost hated to part with it, but she found herself longing for the sight of his face, for the ready smile she always saw there and the desire in his eyes that made her feel so special.

"I'll try," she compromised.

"You have to do better than that."

"Okay, I *will* be reasonable."

"All right." He pulled the shirt off and the bandanna mask went with it. She blinked against the brightness of the room.

He unfastened the front closure of her bra and tossed it aside. Her breasts felt pleasantly heavy and full, and when he took one in his hand, pleasure rippled to every nerve ending. He rubbed a thumb over the already beaded tip and the ripple became a wave.

She rose to wrap her arms around him, needing to share the wonder he made her feel, needing to know that he shared with her the echo of that night five months ago.

"Sin," she whispered, trying to inch his shirt up as he planted kisses along her throat and dipped his tongue into her ear. "I wanted to stay that morning. I did."

"I..." He paused as she pulled the shirt over his head. "I should have made you stay," he said.

She reached to the waistband of his jeans and he stood to accommodate her. She lowered the zipper.

"But I was so sure you were wrong for me," she said, placing her hands against his flat stomach in an apologetic caress. Then she leaned forward to put her lips there.

He put a hand to her hair and held her against him, a shudder of feeling both physical and emotional racking his frame. "I'm perfect for you," he said softly. "You're perfect for me."

He toed off his shoes, then pulled off his jeans and briefs. He put a knee to the bed, wrapped his arms around Bobbi and pulled her with him to the pillows.

The practical side of her nature, fighting through sensation that was swiftly developing from a wave into a tidal surge, felt obliged to remind him, "Nothing . . . is ever perfect."

He looked into her eyes, the dark passion, the ready humor and a shameless wickedness brewing together in his eyes. "I'm going to prove you wrong, Bobbi. Absolutely, unequivocally wrong. Now, pay attention."

He did. In no time at all.

His warm, sure hand swept up the back of her thigh, up over her hip, then down again to stroke a slow, taunting circle over her bottom.

She felt herself turn to warm liquid.

Then he stroked down her thigh again and up the inside, then down the other and up again, finally closing his hand gently but possessively over the mound of her womanhood.

She turned into him and hooked an arm around his waist. He cradled her in his arm and hitched her leg over his hip. They clung together, mouths nibbling, kissing, devouring, hands stroking, exploring, discovering.

The first touch of his fingers inside her brought a little sigh from her at the delicious rightness of it, at the blossom of a memory from that fateful night. It had been as though he knew her, as though he could read her mind and her body. As though she'd been made for him, and he for her.

She felt just that way now as his fingers probed and teased while he held her in the crook of his arm and gave her his complete attention.

His dark eyes looked down into hers as he brought her to the very brink of release, then withdrew to tease her again.

She scraped her fingertips through the side of his hair and reached her lips up for his. "I love you," she whispered, tight with longing and need and the threat of madness. "Love me, Sin. Please."

"Could the wrong man," he asked, his voice husky with his own need and longing, "make you feel like this?"

He brought her to the edge again, then stopped.

She pressed herself closer, pinched his ear. "No. No, he couldn't."

"Then if I'm not the wrong man..." He turned onto his back and pulled her over him. He entered her in a single, smooth stroke and heard her welcoming little sigh, felt her tremble as she closed around him. "...who am I, Bobbi?"

"The right man," she said, knowing it with the personal certainty of accepting a truth. He belonged inside her; she was destined to be a part of him. They were halves of a special whole. "You're the right man, Sin."

He heard the words with satisfaction. He bracketed her waist with his hands and began the sinuous circle that brought her to the edge of fulfillment, then pushed her mercifully over.

On the edge of insanity himself, he still took the pleasure of a moment to watch her gasp and shudder and ride the sensation out, the sun gilding her hair, burnishing her shoulders.

Then he let himself follow her, abandoning all control and reserve to drive her up again so that they spun together in the orbit of the universe, turning and twirling until they were sharpened into a single element composed of two.

They finally drew apart, each amazed that they were able to do so.

She sank onto his chest. He pulled the blankets up over her and turned her onto her side so that she could lie comfortably.

He rubbed a hand gently over her tummy. "You feel all right?" he asked.

She forced her crowded brain to think. "I feel . . . funny."

He rose on an elbow instantly. "What do you mean?"

She kissed his shoulder. "Not that. The baby's fine. I mean I feel different." She hesitated over a word and finally settled on "Giggly." Then laughed just to prove it.

When his eyebrow went up, she giggled even harder. "I know it's juvenile, but I can't help it. I've got it back, and it feels so wonderful."

"Got the giggles back?" he asked in confusion.

"Got the feeling back," she explained. "The happiness. The . . . the family feeling."

"Oh." He relaxed and leaned down to kiss her slowly. "That other side of the sun feeling. You know why, don't you?"

She did. "Because you're the right man."

He rewarded her with another kiss. "Yes. And together we're going to start the Sinclair Cradle on another new and fruitful career. One day one of our descendants will pack up the cradle on his or her moonmobile and there'll be furniture restoration and legal representation out there in the galaxy thanks to our efforts."

She looked up at the beamed ceiling and smiled. "We'll have been the inspiration for space pioneering. I like that."

The sound of an engine in the driveway brought them both bolt upright.

"Who could that be?" Bobbi asked, clutching the blankets to her breast.

Sin was laughing and pulling on his jeans. "The furniture you bought this morning," he said, yanking on his shirt. "I forgot all about them delivering. Stay in bed. Take your nap. I'll find a place for everything."

He headed for the door, his sneakers snagged in the fingers of his right hand. He stopped, blew her a kiss, then pulled the door closed behind him.

Bobbi slowly pulled on her working sweats while listening to the sound of male laughter and the bump and shuffle of furniture being moved.

Well-being sprang into the center of her like a fountain. She belonged to someone and he belonged to her. It didn't matter that it had all come about in a curious way, or that it had taken her a while to decide that what she felt was real. It was. It had become part of her. It was truth.

Finally admitting it to herself was like a dunking in bubble bath. Not only did she feel clean, but fragrant as well.

She slipped into her shoes and went out to supervise the placement of the precious projects that would keep her busy until the baby arrived.

"IT LOOKS LIKE a turn of the century bordello in here," Sin said. He stood in the middle of the shop, his arms wrapped around Bobbi who stood with her back to him.

They'd bought a wicker chair and rocker, a dining table with chipped veneer, several nondescript chairs in desperate need of reupholstering, a dentist's cabinet, a steamer trunk, the baker's table and an old ship's lamp.

"It gives me a great sense of security," she said, her hands rubbing along his forearms. "I love it best when my shop is full of work to be done. 'Course the constant phone calls from the customer asking when the piece will be ready drove me crazy, but now I have the best of both worlds. Lots to do, but no one clamoring for it. And I'm pretty sure I have enough connections to sell it all."

"What's the dentist's cabinet for? All those little drawers wouldn't work for anybody else."

"It would for someone with lots of little things to put in it. Like baby clothes."

"Ah." He kissed her neck. "I'm glad we get to keep something. But if you're going to make a mint off all the rest, then I can leave the firm and you can support me. We can live here and I can fish and write a book of tall fishing yarns.''

Bobbi sighed dreamily. ''Wouldn't that be perfect?''

Sin heard the wistfulness and turned her in his arms. ''You love this place as much as I do,'' he guessed.

''More than you do,'' she corrected. ''I couldn't bear to spend fifty weeks of the year away from here.'' She sighed and looked down at her shoes. ''I know you have to. I just think it'd be great if you didn't.''

''The social strata thing,'' he said.

''I guess.'' She looked up at him and smiled thinly. ''I'm the daughter of a plumber and a motel maid. I put myself through junior college waitressing. I supported Joey and myself by restoring furniture during the day and working for a maid service three evenings a week. I can't even imagine what your *real* life must be like.''

''Would that change anything,'' he asked, ''as long as the *real* me was in it?''

Already she couldn't conceive of life without him. She put her arms around his waist and let her smile widen. ''I guess not.''

He looped his arms around her and she leaned back against his hands. ''May I remind you,'' he said, his tone gently scolding, ''that your best friend, Gina Gallagher, is a member of the group that causes you such concern? And that the two of you have been like sisters for years?''

Bobbi nodded acceptance. ''I know. I know.'' Then she grinned up at him. ''May I remind you that she's now living in a beautiful little community a lot like this one except that it's on the river instead of in the woods?"

He shook his head. "You lose. She and Patrick run a hotel that's often filled with the same southern California upper crust you're afraid to get involved with. And she seems to be doing fine."

Bobbi made a face at him, then leaned her cheek against his shirtfront. "A quiet, country environment would be better for the children."

"Los Angeles has galleries, museums, the Music Center and any number of cultural advantages that would benefit the children."

She sighed, accepting reality. "Maybe we could spend a month here in the summer, instead of just two weeks?"

He hugged her closer. "And the Christmas holidays."

That sounded wonderful. The Christmas holidays. This year she would have them here. That fountain of well-being shot higher as she considered that.

She leaned back to ask him, "What do you want for Christmas?"

"It won't even be Halloween for another month," he laughed.

"I know," she replied, walking him into the kitchen. "But we crafty types have to plan early to get our special projects done. A rolltop desk? A throne chair?"

He smiled down into her face. "I think I'd like the promise that I'll see that happiness in your eyes every day."

"I promise," she said, stopping in the middle of the kitchen to turn and seal the promise with a kiss. She felt at that moment as though her happiness would last into eternity.

The kiss ignited without warning. What began as a tender exchange, a tribute to their discovery of each other, became a testament to the depths of the passion they'd found.

With cautions and constraints finally cast aside, they were like magnetized forces that couldn't be separated without the force of nature drawing them back together.

His tongue teased, his hands roamed, his arms lifted her and then he hesitated.

She lifted her head from his shoulder, languid longing already taking over her body. "What?" she asked vaguely.

He put her on her feet and expelled a groaning breath. "This probably isn't a good idea."

She blinked, temporarily confused. "It's hard to think of it as a bad one."

He laughed softly and leaned down to give her a kiss that he'd intended to be quick. Her lips snared him, however, and he did the job slowly, letting her lure him closer with a hand in the hair at the back of his neck.

Then he pulled her hands away and pushed her a step back. "We've got to go easy on you. Lovemaking is safe, but twice in three hours is probably overdoing it, especially since you've had a little difficulty."

"But I feel fine," she insisted.

He nodded and turned resolutely toward the garage. "And we want to keep you that way. Come on."

She followed with disappointment and reluctance. "We're going for a drive?"

"No, we're going fishing. Poles are in the garage."

"Oh, boy," she said under her breath. "Dead worms and slimy fish. I'm going to love this."

TO BOBBI'S COMPLETE surprise, she did love fishing. For three weeks they'd come to the stream several times a week and spent the early evening sitting on the bank, feet dangling over the edge. She loved the absence of human voices and the scores of natural sounds that filled the silence.

She loved to watch the sun wane. She loved the way Sin always came to her when the sun was down and put her jacket over her shoulders, always punctuating the little duty with a kiss on the side of her neck. She loved the woodsy smell of the fire as he prepared their catch.

She could not remember ever being this happy.

"What're you going to be for Halloween?" she asked Sin, watching from the other side of the fire as he kept the now perfectly fried fish on the sides of the pan and sautéed the fragrant potatoes in the center.

He gave her a quick glance that told her what he thought of costumes. "I gotta be me, Bobbi. No suiting up in someone else's persona."

"That's chicken," she said bluntly, snuggling deeper into her jacket. The nights were quickly growing colder. "You have to wear a costume. The children will love it."

He frowned at her. "What children?"

"The trick or treaters."

"They won't come way out here."

"Yes, they will." She smiled sweetly at him when he looked up to fill the plate she held out to him. "When you dropped me off to get fruit and milk today while you went to the library, I was talking to the clerk about it. She said everyone takes their children to every house, because everyone knows everyone. They don't want anyone to feel left out. Isn't that neat?"

He sent her a grin as he filled his plate. "What're you going to give them? You've already gone through the bag of Snickers we bought last week."

She looked first surprised, then sheepish, then teasingly annoyed. "Spying on me?"

They sat side by side on the bench, plates balanced on their knees. "Not deliberately," he replied. "I went to get one for myself and found only one left."

"So that's what happened to it." She gave him an accusing glance over a forkful of succulent trout. She chewed and swallowed. "I can't believe you saw only one left and took it for yourself."

"I'm selfish through and through," he said with no apparent remorse. "I suppose it's better you find that out now."

She speared a bite of potato and examined it thoughtfully. "You should consider being Dracula for Halloween," she said with a straight face. "He liked to nibble on things, too."

He turned a threatening glance on her, but his eyes were bright with amusement. "Clever. And we'll just drape that orange stuff you bought to reupholster the settee and you can be a pumpkin, you little garbage gut.''

She put a hand defensively to her growing stomach. ''That's the baby, it isn't me.''

''I guess we'll know that for sure when you deliver, won't we?''

''Maybe I won't deliver, just to keep you wondering.''

He shook his head. ''Just like you. Hold everything inside and let everyone wonder what you're up to.''

She choked on a sip from the hot coffee they'd brought in a thermos. She put her cup down and laughed. ''I don't do that. I thought I was very direct.''

''Really?'' he said in a questioning tone. ''You're direct about things you're willing to battle about, but not in things you don't want to discuss.''

''I know where you're going with this,'' she said, spearing two bites of potato on her fork. She'd never in her life had potatoes like the ones he made over a fire. ''A wedding date.''

''I wasn't going anywhere with it,'' he denied, putting the last bite of trout into his mouth. ''You're the one who started it with threats of keeping the baby inside. And anyway, I think the baby'll have something to say about that. Then again, it might choose to stay inside you when it gets wind of the notion that *nobody* will know its name.''

She frowned and concentrated on her food, deliberately misunderstanding him. ''I suppose we should make a decision pretty soon. Maybe we could toss a coin. Your Ariel against my Janeil, your Nicholas against my Travis."

He mimed giving her a sock to the jaw. "Like you don't know I'm talking about the baby's surname."

She tried to fake him out with an innocent stare. "It's your baby. It'll have your name."

Sin met her eyes with a stare that was anything but innocent. "I intend to be married to its mother when that happens."

She leaned back with her coffee and stared out over the stream. "I told you I'd like Gina to stand up for me, and she's in L.A. with her father right now."

Patrick had called the week before with the news that Wyatt Raleigh, Gina's father, had suffered a heart attack while campaigning for a congressional seat, and Gina had flown out to be with him.

"Then why don't we plan to do it the first weekend she's back?"

"Because we don't know when that'll be."

"The date will be understood to be the Saturday of the first weekend after she returns." His voice remained as even as hers, his jaw as square.

"You're pushing me."

He sighed. "Consider yourself lucky. What I'd really like to do is swat you. In fact, that's the first thing I'm going to do once you deliver this baby."

"That settles it." She gathered up their things. "I'm definitely not delivering."

Chapter Ten

To welcome trick or treaters, Sin settled for the old football jersey he'd kept for sentimental reasons and always brought with him to the cabin. Bobbi took him up on the pumpkin idea and made leg holes in the middle of a large square of orange fabric, then gathered the whole thing around her neck with a fat green bow to which she added cutout leaves and curled florist wire for vine. Green tights completed the outfit.

In the window, between two brightly lit jack-o'-lanterns was the plastic pumpkin they'd bought at the church bazaar. It was filled with weeds and fallen oak and maple leaves collected on an afternoon walk along the road.

Children began knocking on the door at dusk. Cars and trucks stopped at the foot of the driveway, unloading pirates, angels, cats, robots, hoboes, mummies, painted ladies and an inordinate amount of turtles wearing masks.

They held out pillowcases, plastic bags, plastic pumpkins, and one resourceful turtle opened a thirty-gallon garbage bag. But to the last child, eyes glowed with the excitement of pretense and the anticipation of a candy supply that would last the week.

"I thought turtles ate worms and snails," Sin teased the ten- or eleven-year-old turtle with the garbage bag. Sin held the bowl of treats while Bobbi dropped some into the sack.

Holding tightly to the boy's free hand was a three- or four-year-old fairy princess carrying a wand. The wand seemed to be more important to her than the plastic bag she'd brought to fill. Bobbi bent over her own awkward tummy and costume to open the bag and drop candy into it.

The girl looked at her with quarter-size velvet-brown eyes, then touched her with the star tip of her wand. "Thank you vewy much," she said.

Bobbi fully expected to disassemble into a column of stardust and turn into a swan.

A broad grin broke under the boy's mask. "That's the California turtle," he replied. "The Oregon turtle eats chocolate and pizza."

"Hmm," Sin said gravely. "Bet that's not good for your shell."

"Well, see," the boy explained, "those guys live in water and sand where you can get worms and snails. We live in sewers."

Sin frowned. "And you can catch chocolate and pizza down there?"

The boy shook his head. "We have it delivered. Later, Dude." He smiled at Bobbi. "Mrs. Dude."

Sin watched until the children joined the adult waiting just behind the arrow of light, then closed the door.

"Cowabunga," he said to Bobbi. "Now, I finally understand you."

She blinked. "Oh?"

"Yes. You're not a Northern Hemisphere Homo Sapien."

"I'm not?"

"No. You're an Oregon turtle that lives on chocolate and pizza."

She gut-punched him. "Let's have coffee and a Snickers bar." They'd bought more to replace those she'd eaten. "I'm starved."

He shook his head. "Sorry."

"Oh, come on, Sinclair," she grumbled. "You're not going to be stuffy on Halloween? A little fairy princess just cast a spell on me. I could turn you into something *awful*."

He didn't appear to feel threatened as he started for the kitchen. "I don't think the spell from a fairy princess would allow you to do magic. That would take a witch."

She followed him to the counter and peered around the refrigerator door while he delved inside.

"Then how do you explain Cinderella?"

He closed the door and looked down at her with a raised eyebrow. "Scuse me?"

"She got a new dress, glass slippers..."

"That was a fairy *godmother,* not a simple princess," Sin replied, working a corkscrew into the top of a bottle. "I think it's a hierarchical thing."

"I think you're full of baloney." She looked closer at the bottle as he reached into an overhead cupboard for glasses. "What is this?"

"Apple cider." He also pulled down a baker's box. "And doughnuts. Traditional Halloween fare. I bought them when I went to town this afternoon and hid them from you."

She wrapped her arms around him, squashing much of her pumpkin front against him. "So, you weren't being stuffy after all."

He looked hurt. "I'm crushed that you thought so."

The doorbell rang, and she pulled out of his arms to answer it.

He caught her wrist. "I'll go," he said. "You pour."

She sighed over his protectiveness. "You're afraid evil doers are going to get me if I go to the door myself?"

He grinned and put a finger to her pumpkin stomach. "No. You have to pick up Cinderella at the stroke of midnight. The castle's quite a way from here."

She chased him threateningly but awkwardly. He was saved at the front door by G.I. Joe and Superman.

"WHAT TIME IS IT?" Bobbi lay curled in Sin's lap in one of the big chairs flanking the fireplace. She'd removed her pumpkin persona and now wore only the tights and the green T-shirt she'd worn under the costume. She'd kicked off her shoes, and now reached a woolly-sock-clad foot toward the fire. They'd polished off the doughnuts and were watching the credits

roll on a TV show. Sin snapped the set off with the remote control.

"I don't know," he said drowsily. "You're laying on
my watch arm. Nine-thirty. Ten. Something like that."

"You think the kids have stopped coming?"

"It's been quite a while since the last one."

She took his earlobe in her teeth. "I just wondered," she whispered, "if you were too full of
doughnuts to be hungry for pumpkin."

The cozy warmth he felt changed to heat in a heartbeat. He took a handful of her hair and pulled her head
back so he could look into her eyes. He saw passion
rising there and let himself dwell for just an instant on
what a miracle this all was. Then he had other things
to think about.

He stood with her in his arms.

"Let's stay by the fire," she coaxed, kissing behind
his ear. "It's so warm down here."

He felt a moment's indecision. "I don't want you to
be uncomfortable."

Her arms around his neck, she put her forehead
against his. "How could I be uncomfortable," she
asked, kissing first one eye, then the other, "wrapped
in your arms?"

Defeated by the question, he set her on her feet in
front of the fire, then went to the stairs for the old quilt
hanging from the railing. He spread it out on the floor
and slipped out of his shoes.

He met Bobbi in the middle of the quilt, and took
her weight as they sank to their knees.

"You're sure you're still feeling all right?" he asked, pulling her to him and thinking it amazing that the pleasure of simply holding her never diminished for him. He loved the way she leaned into him, relaxed against him, gave herself over to him with all the confidence of a woman who knew she was loved and would be cared for.

She was ardent and eager and it would take a stronger man than he to resist her.

"I feel better than I've ever felt," she insisted, already wrestling with his jersey.

He raised his arms to help her pull it off, then removed her T-shirt and bra. He framed her face in his hands and just looked at her, needing to slow himself down, to assure himself that he could take care with her. She wound her arms around his neck and looked back, her eyes alive with love and desire and a sweetness that had always been there, but now seemed to be growing along with her pregnancy.

"I love you," she said.

He felt the simple words like a stroke on his face. It was the first time she'd said them without prompting, without responding to his declaration.

"I love *you*," he replied. He wrapped an arm around her and tipped her backward, bracing a hand on the quilt to ease her down.

Her mounded abdomen rose above her like a little hill. He tugged the tights past it and leaned down to kiss her and the child contained inside her.

He felt the baby bump against his cheek and he raised his head to look into her smiling face. "This child is already making sure it gets its share of attention.''

He put his hand over her and the baby moved against it again, seeming to ripple across the width of it as though it had turned, or swung a leg the perimeter of its small enclosure.

Sin thought he'd never experienced anything as magical as the touch of life from ''the other side.'' The unborn communicating with the experienced and jaded to make everything seem fresh and new.

He tugged Bobbi's tights off, removed his shoes and jeans and briefs and lay down beside her, turning her onto her side, facing him. ''It's beginning to feel,'' he said, stroking a hand along her side, ''as though we're making love in the presence of a voyeur.''

She laughed and planted soft kisses along his jawline. ''Maybe this is what they really mean by a ménage à trois.''

Then her hands began to move over him in rapid, artful play carried out in deadly earnest.

He responded in kind, trying to wrest the initiative from her. But she resisted, inching her lower body away from him as she wrapped him in both hands and took him to the edge of insanity.

It occurred to him in a little corner of his mind still operating on a nonsensory level that they did just this every day they were together. One tried to assume control of the relationship from the other. He wanted to marry and she fought him. She wanted to be free to make her decision once she held the baby in her arms, and he was damned if his baby was going to come into this world to a single mother.

That particular argument was still in a stalemate. This one, he determined, forcing his mind to function as well as his body, was about to take a serious turn.

He snaked a long arm out, cupped her hip in his hand and pulled her closer.

"Who am I?" he asked. Her head moved a little frantically on the arm with which he pillowed her. "Open your eyes and tell me who I am."

She lifted light lashes to reveal eyes now as green as the woods behind the house—and as inviting. "You're the right man," she said, leaning up to wrap her arms around his neck, to force her body against his malingering hand. "The right man."

He entered her and gave her all the love he held. She wrested it from every hidden little corner in his being. She drew out every nuance of feeling he hadn't even known he was hoarding, waiting to bestow it on the woman who would cherish it and him because of the person he was.

He felt her shudders of fulfillment, then released his own. The space they occupied was suddenly so hot and so bright, he thought that loving her was like embracing the sun.

Bobbi couldn't quite grasp what was happening to her. As pleasure went on and on, rippling around her in ever-widening circles she felt the final crumbling of all old barriers.

It had only a little to do with Sin's wonderful lovemaking. It had everything to do with the tender, yet possessive way he held her, the gentle passion he lavished on her, the somehow reverent confidence with which he touched her.

Locked in his embrace as they came down slowly from a mutual high, Bobbi knew without a fragment of a doubt that she could no longer live without him. She could go physically from day to day, she would be able to support herself and the baby, but a world without him would be no world at all.

Sin lay back and groaned. "You're going to make me old before my time, woman," he said, reaching behind him to the pile of their clothes. He yanked on a sleeve of his sweater and dragged it to him.

He propped up on an elbow to pull it over her head. She sat up to help him pull it down over her protruding stomach. Then he pulled the quilt over the bottom half of her and over himself.

"I can't believe you spent most of the day in your shop," he went on in teasing admiration, "skipped your nap to finish your costume and still have the stamina to curl my toes."

"I'm from good peasant stock," she said, nuzzling her nose in his throat. "You're a hybrid. It's all in the genetic makeup."

"It's in my good nutrition plan."

"Then how come you're groaning and I'm not? We eat the same things."

He sighed guiltily. "You're having a corrupting effect on me. I had two Snickers today and two doughnuts. Your body's used to the invasion of sugar and cholesterol—mine isn't."

"What about November 28?" Bobbi dropped the question casually into the middle of their frivolous banter.

Sin missed the significance of it. He shifted lazily, running a hand down her back, fascinated with the sinuous line of it even in her pregnancy. "Thanksgiving? What about it?"

"It's the Saturday after," she replied.

He kissed her forehead and thought he really should get her up to bed. She might get chilled lying here. But wrapped around each other they formed a comfortable little cocoon of warmth and he hated to disturb it. "Saturday after Thanksgiving," he murmured into her hair. "We'll be in Candle Bay with Patrick and Gina. We'll drive back Sunday."

She kissed his collarbone and held her breath. "Want to come back married?"

He heard her pose the question, but he didn't believe it. Then he felt as though someone had shaken him and left him stunned. He'd begun to believe the only way he'd ever get her to agree to get married would be to sedate her once the baby was born and fly to some country that didn't require the bride to be conscious to be married.

He had to give himself a moment to answer. It had been important to him from the beginning to assume responsibility for her and the baby. But now that he knew her, really *knew* her, it had become imperative that their lives be permanently connected.

"Yes," he replied calmly. He was afraid a strong reaction would frighten her. "I believe I'd like that."

"We'll have to get health certificates."

"We have them. Dr. Fletcher did them for me right after he saw you that first time. He examined me while you were having your ultrasound."

Bobbi folded her arms on Sin's chest and looked wryly into his eyes. "You were that sure I'd come around."

"No," he admitted honestly. "I just knew I wasn't going to let you go." He reached up to brush her hair back. It was growing longer, and she'd taken to wearing it in soft, loose curls. It sparkled around her head in the firelight like a halo. "You've finally decided surrender is wiser than futile struggle?"

She smiled and pinched his chin. "I think you have so spoiled me that I know I couldn't possibly get along without all this care and cosseting." She leaned up to kiss it, her eyes growing grave. "And my life would seem very empty without you, Sinclair, so I'm going to trust you with it. But you'll have to trust me with yours."

"I did that the day I picked you up at the hospital to bring you here," he said. Then he couldn't remain calm a moment longer. The emotion he felt had to have expression or he would self-destruct.

He squeezed her close, relishing the feel of the still-taut tips of her breasts against his chest, the roundness of their baby pressing just under his ribs, the way she always hitched her leg against him when he held her, as though she needed to be closer still. He kissed her soundly, trying to transfer to her all the passion and power he felt in their union.

"I'm yours, Bobbi, forever."

November

"You're going to have the hotel dining room *cater* dinner tomorrow?" Sin looked in dismay at their hostess.

Sin and Bobbi sat in the dining room of Patrick and Gina Gallagher's Queen Anne home in Candle Bay, at the mouth of the Columbia River. The house sat on a knoll overlooking the Candle Bay Inn, a hotel that had been in Patrick's family for several generations. Buttercup sat on the back porch, gnawing on a bone from the hotel's kitchen.

Gina, small and dark, and as pregnant as Bobbi, looked back at Sin without a trace of guilt. "I'm going to be a bridesmaid on Saturday," she said. "I'm not going to appear before the minister looking like a hag because I've slaved over Thanksgiving dinner. Patrick has a wonderful chef. You'll enjoy his cooking— trust me."

"But..."

"Sinclair!" Bobbi, who was sitting beside him, backhanded him on the arm. "Don't be ungrateful," she said. She turned to their friends and explained indulgently, "He thinks anything frozen, out of a can, or prepared by someone else is illegal. He has to buy it from an organic farmer, broil or stir-fry it in canola oil, then eat it under a full moon in a graveyard after it's been blessed."

Laughter erupted as her almost sensible scenario took a ridiculous turn. Sin frowned fiercely at her and she giggled without remorse as she put her arms around him and kissed his cheek.

"My point," he said, turning a threatening look on Gina and Patrick who subsided with difficulty, "was nothing against your restaurant's five-star rating, but about our abuse of the integrity of the holiday. We're supposed to be getting together to share what we have in gratitude for a bountiful harvest."

Gina blinked at Sin. "I have one pot of chives on my windowsill."

Patrick turned to his wife, desperately trying to hold back a grin. "Will you straighten up?" he scolded. To Sin he said, "I apologize. She's difficult under the best of circumstances, but when she thinks she's being funny, or when she has an appreciative audience . . ." He indicated Bobbi who choked into a napkin. "I'm sure you understand. You seem to have the same problem."

Sin sighed with forbearance. Then he wrapped both arms around Bobbi in a restrictive rather than a romantic manner and shook her gently. Gina, he fixed with a grim glare. "I'm going to try this one more time," he said.

Gina leaned back in her chair and folded her arms, assuming an attentive manner. "Go for it, Pilgrim," she said.

Bobbi dissolved into laughter again and Sin put a hand over his eyes. Patrick put his over Gina's mouth and said in a strangled tone, "Go ahead, Sin. You have *my* attention."

Bobbi put a fist to her trembling lips, but couldn't hide the laughter in her eyes. She cleared her throat and said with faint composure, "Mine, too. Go on."

"I was going to say," Sin put in quickly, while he could, "that the four of us will soon be harvesting the finest crop nature has to offer." He rubbed a hand lovingly over Bobbi's abdomen.

She melted against him, laughter leaving her, her whole demeanor suddenly soft and unabashedly that of a woman in love.

Patrick dropped his hand from Gina's mouth as she turned to look into his eyes, her own filled with the love and pride reflected in his.

"If anyone should be grateful," Sin went on, pointing around the table, "it's us. So, if you promise not to give me any more flack about it, I'm going to the market right now to buy a turkey and all the fixings. I *can* count on all of you for a little help with preparations?"

Bobbi squeezed his middle. "Of course, darling."

"You bet," Gina agreed.

Patrick stood. "I'll drive you. We'll go to my butcher and grocer."

Bobbi and Gina cleared away the coffee cups after Sin and Patrick left.

"What happened to the playboy bon vivant?" Gina asked. "Sin positively radiates the glow of fatherhood. How did you do that?"

Bobbi shrugged a shoulder. "He seems to have done it himself."

"When the two of you came up for Memorial Day weekend," Gina said, stuffing the cups into the dishwasher and closing the door, "all you did was argue. You couldn't stand to be within half a mile of each other."

Bobbi leaned her weary back against the counter as Gina went to the refrigerator and opened the freezer door. "I was furious with him. After the night of your wedding, I was awestruck by what we'd shared and *he* hadn't even called. Then when he did, I was thrilled—until he made a point of telling me Patrick had insisted he call me about flying up with him to visit you for the weekend. He hurt my feelings."

"I suspect he didn't call and was so impatient with you while the two of you were here," Gina said, pulling a box out of the freezer, "because you were getting to him. According to Patrick, no woman ever got to Sin before you. He loved 'em and left 'em."

"He sure got to me," Bobbi said, frowning down at her shoes, or where she knew her shoes would be if she were able to see beyond her stomach.

"So, here we are," Gina said, leaning against the counter beside her, her abdomen protruding as far as Bobbi's. "Two once single and independent career women from L.A. now tied to two gorgeous but possessive, single-minded males with latent cavemen tendencies."

They stared across the kitchen together, contemplating their fates.

"You sorry?" Gina asked Bobbi.

"Not for a minute," Bobbi replied. "You?"

"Nope. Unless you consider that Patrick's always on me about the junk I like to eat."

Bobbi laughed. "Sin, too. I was exaggerating only a little about the organic farmer, canola oil stuff."

Gina nodded. "So here. There're about five hundred calories in it, but they'll probably all go to making the baby stronger and healthier." She handed Bobbi an ice-cream bar. "Hurry, before they get back."

IN THE WARM, HUMID kitchen, Sin, Bobbi, Patrick and Gina moved around in colliding orbits from counter to refrigerator to stove to chopping block. Each wore a green apron emblazoned with the Candle Bay Inn logo—traditional script in a semicircle with a candle for the "I."

Sin moved from one assistant to the next as complaints and concerns arose. "The gravy's lumpy!" "How long do I bake the rolls?" "Does the turkey look done to you?"

"Remind me not to go in the restaurant business with you guys," Sin said, laying foil over the scorched legs of the turkey Gina had been assigned to watch. "I've never seen such blatant incompetence."

Patrick, who was putting a large pot of potatoes on to boil, laughed. "Wolfgang Puck couldn't afford to go into business with these two," Patrick said, turning the burner on and wiping his hands on his apron as Bobbi and Gina turned to him with injured frowns.

"They'd eat you out of everything and burn what was left."

Gina raised an eyebrow at Bobbi. "I'd really prefer to be in the living room sipping cider and eating those water chestnut and bacon things Sin made, wouldn't you?"

"Quite." Bobbi made a production of removing her apron and handed the knife with which she'd been slicing tomatoes to Sin. "Call us when it's time to eat."

"With you it's always time to eat."

Bobbi sighed at him. "I could rethink this wedding, you know."

He gave her a confident grin and leaned down to kiss her. "No, you couldn't. Get out of here and go put your feet up."

Gina looked at him hopefully. "Me, too?"

"Please," he replied dryly. Then with a smile that belied the abuse he pointed to the refrigerator. "Don't forget the hors d'oeuvres."

"Me, too?" Patrick asked.

Sin glared at him. "You're not pregnant. Get the pies out of the freezer and whip the cream for later."

Patrick stalked to the refrigerator. "Getting a little autocratic, aren't you?" he asked with feigned ill-humor.

"Of course not," Sin replied, then cast him an over the shoulder grin. "But hum a few bars of 'Hail to the Chief' while you're working, will you?"

"'*It's A Wonderful Life*'?" Sin asked in disbelief. He leaned over the back of the sofa where Bobbi and

Gina sat side by side watching the vintage Christmas movie. He poured coffee into the mug each held. "Thanksgiving isn't even over yet."

"Turn that off and turn on the replay of the game!" Patrick shouted from the kitchen.

"Big talker," Sin shouted back. "It's two against one out here!"

"Ha!" Patrick returned. "The game'd be over before either one of them could get off the sofa to fight you!"

Gina turned to Bobbi. "I'm sorry. I don't know what to say. He grows more difficult every day."

"Sin, too, only he made such a wonderful dinner, I suppose we have to forgive him." She leaned back to offer him an upside-down kiss. "Thanks for the coffee. And dinner was wonderful. You're so clever."

He put a modest hand to his heart. "I know. Pat's obnoxious and I'm clever. It's kind of how it's always been."

Patrick came out of the kitchen, still wearing his apron. "I heard that," he said.

Gina reached over the back of the sofa for his hand. "Don't be upset, sweetheart. I think you're very clever at being obnoxious."

Patrick folded his arms over his still-aproned chest and looked at Sin. "Don't you think we've taken just about enough of this abuse?"

"Definitely," Patrick replied, still holding the coffeepot. "What do you propose we do about it?"

"I think we should take them dancing at the Inn." He pointed through the living room window at the small cluster of lights in the corner that indicated the dance pavilion right on the water.

Gina smiled in approval, then turned to Bobbi with a frown of concern. "Do you feel up to it? Please be honest if you don't."

"I'm fine," Bobbi said. Actually she was ecstatic with the warmth of Sin's love embracing her and the wonderful comfort of the Gallaghers' friendship. She grinned up at Sin. "And I did bring my pink dress."

"You're sure you're not too tired?" Sin asked. "No one's going to be upset if you are."

"*I'm* going to be upset if anyone asks me that again," she retorted, then tried to push herself to her feet. The protrusion of the baby didn't allow her the momentum she needed and she fell back. She and Gina giggled together.

"Told you," Patrick said to Sin as he went around the sofa to lend her a hand. "You could have switched to the game no problem."

"YOU LOOK GOOD ENOUGH to eat," Sin said, holding Bobbi to him on the dance floor. Stars and lights from the boats on the river and Astoria across the bay winked through the blackness beyond the glass walls of the pavilion. The band played something torchy and slow.

Bobbi leaned into him, feeling his warmth and strength surround her as he leaned slightly over her to accommodate her stomach. "It'd be like getting your second helping with your first," she joked. "I'm beginning to feel like a beached whale." Then she tipped her head back to look up into his eyes. "Only I don't tonight. Tonight I feel glamorous." Her forehead furrowed in surprise. "Why do you suppose that is? I ate more turkey than you did."

Sin laughed and kissed her cheek and pushed her head back to his shoulder. "You feel glamorous because you are breathtaking. I like what you did to your hair."

She and Gina had done each other's hair as though they were high school girls rather than married women expecting their first offspring. She'd swept Gina's into a high mound dripping with curls and ruffly bangs. Gina had given her a sideswept do that *did* lend her an air of razzle-dazzle usually foreign to her casual appearance.

Sin felt her deeper inclination toward him, felt every luscious curve of her press into every part of him eager to accept her and decided quickly that their hasty escape was the better part of valor.

He glanced at Patrick and Gina, leaning moodily against each other and swaying to the music, looking as though they were anchored to the spot and had no intention of moving anytime soon.

"Want to go back to the house?" Sin asked softly in Bobbi's ear.

"Yes," she whispered back, then inclined her head toward their friends. "But I hate to make them leave if they're not ready."

Sin glanced up at Patrick, trying to decide between indulging a burning personal need and exerting the common courtesy of a houseguest. Patrick reached into his pocket while still holding Gina against him and dangled a ring of keys on his index finger.

Sin took Bobbi's hand and led her the few steps across the floor to take the keys from Patrick.

"You read my mind," Sin said.

Patrick grinned. "Not the details, don't worry."

"You don't mind?"

"Of course not. See you guys for breakfast."

"DID YOU AND PATRICK use this room as young men on break from school?" Bobbi asked from the middle of the brass bed covered in a blue woven blanket. They'd removed and folded the old quilt that covered it and Sin, naked, was reaching up to the closet shelf for a down comforter.

"No, this house was empty then," he said. "Patrick's grandfather lived at the Inn and used to put us up in one of the best rooms on the top floor. In exchange, we waited tables or crewed on the charter boats."

The comforter tucked under one arm, he flipped off the closet light and went to the foot of the bed. He shook out the puffy fabric and Bobbi caught the top edge to pull it into place. "I always preferred coming here to going home. Patrick's parents died very young, but his grandfather was wonderful to me. He used to have the chef make cookies and fudge and send them to us at school."

He flipped off the hand-painted oil lamp wired to use electricity, and climbed into the big soft bed. The sensation after a long, fun-filled but busy day drew a hedonistic sigh from him.

When Bobbi moved into his arms the sigh became a groan of pleasure so complete it was almost pain. It clutched at him on every level—spiritual, emotional and physical. He'd never been one to question the good fortune that came his way—he'd worked hard for much of it, and what he'd inherited he'd maneuvered to parlay into even more.

But Bobbi had been a simple trick of fate—the curious result of his efforts to help Patrick get a loan that had resulted also in getting him a wife. And getting Patrick married to that wife had brought Bobbi on the scene as Gina's maid-of-honor. What an unlikely chain of events had brought him to this place of happiness and fulfillment. When he thought about it in those terms, it seemed truly fragile.

He hugged her to him harder than he'd intended to. She gasped a protest and he kissed her apologetically. "Sorry," he whispered. "Didn't want you to get away."

She wriggled against him, banishing his concerns, raising his already alert libido. "I don't want to go away. Why? Are you getting cold feet?"

He slipped a hand between her knees and swept it up her thigh to close it over the warm heart of her. He felt her little sigh of contentment, then the stillness that always came over her as she awaited his next move.

"There is nothing cold about me," he said, nipping her ear as she turned her face into his shoulder. He slipped a finger inside her and felt her tense and tighten, heard almost immediately the quickening of her breath. "There hasn't been since the day of Pat and

Gina's wedding when we were first introduced and you smiled at me.''

She hitched a leg against him and little cries began to punctuate her puffs of breath. This time he couldn't tease her.

He pulled her astride him, lifted her carefully and slipped into her with the ease of perfect belonging. The shudders overtook her immediately, and he prolonged them with attentive strokes to her full breasts and the very firm mound of their baby. He reached behind her to stroke her back and bottom, and she leaned forward onto him as much as her abdomen would allow.

Then she began to move on him, a graceful, contemporary symbol of fertility caught in the orbit of the world they'd made. Pleasure overwhelmed him and he slipped over the edge, falling helplessly through the universe she'd opened to him.

Chapter Eleven

"Do you, Barbara take Paul for your wedded husband? To have and to..."

Bobbi heard the questions and responded to them with a sense of unreality. She'd been through this little ritual seven short months ago, only then the names involved had been Patrick and Regina.

She'd thought Gina was crazy because she'd known Patrick only a few days, and was marrying him as a condition of her father's loan to him. She'd been sure the whole thing would blow up in her friend's face and leave her life a bigger mess than it had been when she'd decided to take such a foolhardy step.

But Patrick and Gina's story had had a fairy-tale ending.

Now she stood beside the proverbial prince who lavished love and attention on her. She'd just heard him reply firmly, "I will," when asked to vow to do those things.

Sin was just relieved that it was finally happening.

Bobbi made her vows quietly but with believable sincerity, if with a trace of awe.

Now there was no going back. Relief filled him.

Sin put a broad gold band intricately carved with roses on Bobbi's finger. She slipped the broader, matching band on his and looked up into his eyes. Quiet possession burned in them.

There were hugs and tears and congratulations after the simple ceremony. Then Patrick drove them back to the house, taking an unexpected turn at the last moment onto the grounds of the inn, then farther to the dock where the pleasure boats were moored.

"Ah..." Sin said, ducking his head to look at their surroundings through the back seat windows. "Patrick, it's nice of you to think I'd like to go fishing, but this *is* my wedding day. Bobbi might have other ideas about..."

Patrick braked to a stop at the edge of the dock. "God, Sinclair," he said, grinning at him through his rearview mirror. "Get you near a body of water and all your mind can conclude is that you're going fishing. That's not the plan at all."

He got out of the car and came around to help Bobbi out, then shook his head at Sin as he followed.

"You're so unimaginative," he said gravely. "Now that you're a married man, you have to become more creative in your thinking. Living with a woman day after day, you're going to have to be faster on your mental feet if you expect to keep up. Their thought processes don't follow conventional paths. You—"

Gina silenced him with an elbow in the ribs. "Our wedding gift to you is a night's cruise on the *River Star*." She swept an arm toward a small, sleekly beautiful yacht. Bobbi remembered being told when she visited in May that the inn used it for special parties and chartered it for special guests. "We were hoping the weather would hold out. No rain or wind in sight for two days. Just cold and clear."

"It'll have you back in time for breakfast in the morning," Patrick said, "and you can head for home right on schedule."

"We had your bags put aboard while we were at the church. Don't worry about Buttercup. We'll spoil her for you tonight."

Bobbi stared at the yacht in amazement. "I've never been on anything but the Catalina Steamer."

"Then, follow Sin aboard," Patrick leaned down to give her a hug. "You're in for a treat. See you two in the morning." He shook hands with Sin. "I know you've won sailing trophies, Sin, but I've told the captain about the time you tacked right into the Power Squadron's cocktail party in Long Beach Harbor and sent two society matrons overboard. So, don't try to take the helm, okay. Keep yourself busy with other things."

"I rescued the matrons, if you'll recall," Sin said over his shoulder as Patrick pushed them to the rail of the yacht where the captain waited to help them aboard.

Patrick nodded. "I know, but one lost her purse in the water, and the other, the abbreviated top of a bathing suit that apparently had never been intended for the water. I believe it dissolved, or something.''

Sin leapt aboard and turned to help Bobbi up. The captain leaned out to lend a hand.

''John Regent,'' he said when they were safely on deck. He shook hands with Sin, then with Bobbi. He was a tall, elegantly mustached man Bobbi guessed to be in his early sixties, but obviously fit under his sailing whites. ''Why don't you two lay aft, and we'll be under way. I'll send coffee to you.'' Regent waved at Gina and Patrick.

''Take good care of them for you, sir!'' he called.

''Do that, John,'' Patrick replied, waving back. ''Have fun. Relax!''

The captain disappeared, and there was the sudden thrum of a powerful engine.

''Why don't we what?'' Bobbi asked as Sin wrapped his arm around her to steady her.

''Lay aft,'' Sin said. ''Go to the back of the boat.''

''Oh. Why is it the minute you get on a boat, English no longer applies?''

''Grump, grump. Wave.'' Patrick and Gina, still waving, receded as the yacht glided farther out into the river, then turned in the direction of Astoria.

''I CAN'T BELIEVE THIS,'' Bobbi said dreamily. Night had fallen, and they'd dropped anchor in a little cove upriver. They'd spent the early evening hours eating sautéed scallops and salad in the most elegant dining room Bobbi had ever expected to find afloat, complete with fine china, silver service, candlelight and an attentive young waiter who'd apparently promised Patrick to see that his guests wanted for nothing.

Now Bobbi reclined between Sin's legs on a chaise on the afterdeck. Wrapped in a blanket, they watched a freighter rumble by. It was brightly lit and somehow inviting.

"Isn't that romantic?" Bobbi asked. "Did you ever want to run away to sea?"

"Yes," he admitted, kissing her temple. "But not on a freighter, on a beautiful little Swedish cutter."

"Is that what you have now?"

He nodded. "Just bought it. Used to be a herring smack a century ago. A friend's restoring the cabin for me in Newport."

"But you have to do all the work on a sailboat. There's no one to serve you dinner by candlelight."

His arms tightened around her. "I thought *you* could do that for me."

"Oh, you did?" She pinched his knee. "Think again. I'll have a baby to contend with."

"Well, on a boat, Bobbi," he said seriously, "everyone has to pull his or her weight."

"Actually..." She sighed and let the word trail out on the night wind. "There are a few duties I'd be willing to take on."

"What're those?"

She tried to turn herself to look at him, but she had reached the point in her pregnancy where graceful movement of any kind was impossible. Sin sat up and with an arm across her back and one under her knees, turned her sideways to cradle her in one arm, then re-arranged the blanket over her.

She snuggled into him suggestively. "I'd like to be the person who takes care of the captain's personal things."

"There isn't much room on a boat for personal belongings," he replied innocently. "I don't bring..."

Under cover of the blanket, she slipped her fingers inside the sweats he'd changed into for sitting on deck in the chilly night air. "I mean," she said softly, "*personal* things."

"Oooh," he said, drawing out the word.

"Want to go to our bunk," she asked, drawing her hand back and playfully batting her eyelashes, "and talk over the details of the job?"

"I don't think so," he replied, tugging at the sweats she also wore. "I want to stay right here." He opened his mouth over hers while his hand pulled the pants clear of her bottom.

"Sin!" she whispered, looking surreptitiously around them as she struggled faintly against him. "We are not alone."

"Fish don't have this much fun," he said, taunting her with the lightest touch of his fingertips from her knee to the juncture of her torso. With satisfaction he felt her tremble. "They don't care what we're doing. They probably wouldn't even recognize it for what it is."

"I'm not talking about fish," she said, reaching for his teasing hands. He evaded her. "I'm talking about the captain and the steward."

"They're having a very intent game of chess," Sin said, holding both her hands in the one he had wrapped around her waist. The other had swept down all barriers and was doing devilish things to her. "They won't be thinking about us. And, right now, I don't want to think about them."

She couldn't form the will or the words to protest. Her brain was addled and the entire focus of her concentration was on his hand and the delicious madness to which it brought her.

She writhed in his arms, uttering a wanton little cry. He freed her hands and covered her mouth.

"Shh!" he cautioned in a whisper, his grin flashing. "And don't wriggle or we'll go over the side in this chaise! That'll look great on Patrick's S.A.I.F. report."

She was amazed and mystified to find that laughter heightened fulfillment.

Sin laughed with her, then sobered suddenly as it hit him that she was his—not just in his own mind, but in hers, and according to the laws of God and man. It was powerful stuff, and he felt it surge through him like a charge.

Gina looked up at him, the moon-colored curls around her face dancing in the strengthening wind. Her eyes ran over his face with a slow care that paralyzed him. At that same moment, her hands closed over him. For an instant she had him ensnared. Her hands made him wild and he could only look back into her eyes in a kind of anxious delirium. Then the power within him bucked for freedom.

He eased her over him and gave it free rein. With no room to move, they simply clung together, straining against and into each other, bound by the energy they created.

Sin felt part of the night, as hot as a star, as wild as the ocean and every bit as deep.

Bobbi felt like the wind, strong and perfumed and racing to unknown places.

There was a distant blast of a horn as a ship passed off the port side. Bobbi raised her head in alarm.

"It's all right." Sin tightened his grip on her. "Lie still," he said, a smile in his voice. "We're going to get her backwash in a minute."

Bobbi, her senses drugged by his lovemaking and the fact that her body still held his, wondered why he found another ship's backwash amusing when it hit them—and she understood.

Waves rolled under them. The little yacht rose and fell and so did they, still locked together. Bobbi found herself clinging to Sin and crying out in amazement as eddies of pleasure broke over her all over again, echoing the waves rolling under them from the passing ship. Sin had known it would happen.

Bobbi heard the footsteps and groaned. She tried to back away, to free Sin, but he held her in place.

"Hush," he whispered.

"Mr. Sinclair?" the captain asked in a voice quiet with concern.

"Yes, Captain," Sin replied. He stroked a hand gently over Bobbi's hair.

"Did I hear the lady cry out? Is she all right? She isn't . . . ?"

Sin laughed softly and shook his head. "No, she isn't about to turn us into midwives. She dozed and had a bad dream. She's fine."

"It's getting cold out here. If you'd like to take her inside, the steward will bring you a brandy and cocoa for the lady."

"Thank you," Sin replied. "But give us just a few minutes. I was . . ." There was a pause. Bobbi, her face covered by the blanket, scrunched her eyes tightly. "I was enjoying the moment," Sin finally said.

"I understand, sir."

Bobbi was grateful the captain missed the irony in his voice. He took the statement at its face value. What newly married man wouldn't enjoy holding his wife on a deck chair on a yacht in the moonlight?

The captain, of course, had no idea what had been going on under the blanket.

"You *devil*," Bobbi whispered at him as the captain walked away, whistling.

"I was being perfectly honest," he replied innocently, as they helped each other readjust clothing. "Weren't *you* enjoying the moment?"

She gave him a scolding look, then collapsed against him, laughing helplessly, when she remembered how she'd felt when she'd heard the captain's footsteps approach.

"Maybe we'd better go down to the cabin now," Sin suggested, laughing with her.

"Maybe we'd better."

BOBBI WAS SNUGGLED to Sin's side against the railing of the *River Star* as it crossed Candle Bay and turned toward the far shore. It was early afternoon, and the hotel began to take on shape and detail under the bright sun as they drew closer. Bobbi was thinking that life with a man who had a passion for sailing might be even better than she'd imagined, when the man in question straightened suddenly against the rail and let out a low, groaning, "Oh, no!"

Bobbi stiffened in alarm beside him. "What?"

He frowned at the dock they approached. Figures were visible. Bobbi could make out Gina's pregnant form, and those of a man and woman standing on either side of her.

"My parents," Sin said.

Bobbi squinted at the silver-haired pair growing ever clearer as the yacht drew closer. They looked like an advertisement for chic among the older set.

"They're very handsome," she said.

He nodded agreement, still frowning. "Yes, they are."

"Do they know? About..." She gestured from him to her.

"No. And they don't know about the baby."

Great, she thought. *This gets me off on the right foot.* "Are they going to hate me?"

He pulled her closer and kissed the top of her head, still frowning as the yacht slipped in beside the dock. "No. They'll love you because you belong to me."

"I'm confused."

"They love me. They just never had time for me."

She frowned up at him. "If they love you, why are you upset?"

He sighed moodily. "I don't know. Habit."

Bobbi wasn't sure what she expected of Sin's parents, but what they seemed to be wasn't it. After his few but angry remarks about his childhood and his parents' inattentiveness, she was surprised by their effusion at the sight of him, and the tears in his mother's eyes when she wrapped her arms around Bobbi and unabashedly admired her pregnancy.

"Connie Britain," Janice Sinclair explained, "the wife of Dr. Britain who saw you in emergency, was in London visiting her sister and we bumped into each other at Kensington Place after antique shopping. She congratulated me on becoming a grandmother." She cast a mildly scolding glance at Sin. "As it was the first we'd heard about it, we thought we'd better come home and find out what's going on."

"We've been all the way to the boonies and back trying to track you down," Douglas Sinclair said.

Sin looked as though he'd been cloned from him, Bobbi thought. Father and son were the same height, built very similarly and each looked at the other with a wary kind of respect. They'd never been friends, she concluded.

"Sorry. You seem to have survived the *boonies,*" Sin said, his slight emphasis on the word suggesting he'd taken exception to it.

Bobbi did find it hard to think of Gold Grove as the back of beyond. To her, it was the heart of everything. But in the older man's defense, she thought it might seem like the edge of nowhere to someone who did business in the glitzy capitals of the world.

Douglas studied Sin for a moment with an edge of impatience, then turned to give Bobbi a hug. "How are you feeling? I understand you had some problems in the beginning."

Bobbi explained briefly and nondramatically about the condition that had led her and Sin to the hospital emergency room.

Douglas nodded. He and Janice flanked Bobbi and began to lead her toward a long black limousine next to which a short, muscular man in chauffeur's uniform stood.

She looked over her shoulder to see that Gina had linked her arm in Sin's and they were following along.

"Don't feel badly about being ignored," Gina said quietly to Sin. "Bobbi is cuter than you are, and she *is* carrying their grandchild."

Sin shook his head as he studied the trio being helped into the limo. "I can't imagine why they're so interested. They never left a business deal to come home to see me."

"Maybe they've mellowed and matured," Gina suggested. "I grew up almost the same way you did. My father was around, he just never noticed me. He had his own priorities. Then one day—just a few weeks ago, in fact—he woke up in a hospital room after a heart attack and realized that contracts and a seat in congress aren't the sum total of what life is all about." She shrugged a shoulder. "He now finds me fascinating. He calls me often, and plans to come up when the baby's born.''

Sin's frown of confusion deepened. "But my parents haven't had a brush with death.''

"No, they've had a brush with life," she said gently, gesturing toward Janice adjusting Bobbi's seat belt around her protruding abdomen. "I imagine it can be as powerful when you come to a point where you begin to think things over. I'll wager they know they missed out on a lot with you, and they don't want to make the same mistake with their grandchild.''

"So, I'm supposed to just let them back in?''

"Why not? What do you have to lose? You have the absolute greatest woman in the world for a wife, and you're going to have one of the world's two most brilliant babies.'' She patted her tummy, leaving little doubt as to which baby was the second genius. "You can afford to be generous.''

With everyone else in the limo, Sin stopped Gina a few feet away and grinned down at her. "If I ever convert to polygamy," he said, "would you like to change your name from Gallagher to Sinclair?''

She giggled. "Why don't we just start a commune and all live together?''

"Because that would include Patrick.''

The chauffeur cleared his throat. Sin and Gina looked up.

"Sometime today would be nice, Mr. Sin,'' the man said. "But, then, you never were one for punctuality. Waited for you two hours after your trumpet lesson one afternoon.''

With a sudden laugh, Sin went forward and offered the man his hand. "Baldwin. How the hell are you?"

"Good, sir. How are you?"

"Wonderful. Have you met Mrs. Gallagher?"

"I've met everyone," Baldwin assured him. "We're just waiting on you—as usual."

"You waited two hours," Sin said, helping Baldwin put Gina into the car, "because I didn't go to my trumpet lesson."

"I know. You went to the pool hall on Spring Street. Always had a creative approach to everything." With Gina in the middle seat of the limousine, Baldwin held the door to the front passenger seat open for Sin. "Must say your style's improving. That's a beautiful lady."

"Thank you, Baldy. Where are we going?"

"Back to the house for the ladies to freshen up. Then Mr. Gallagher's expecting you all in the hotel dining room at six."

Sin glanced into the back where Bobbi and his parents were talking as if they were old friends. He sighed. "Maybe I'll hang out with you tonight, Baldy."

"Good, sir," Baldwin said, winking just before he closed the door. "Because I'm invited, too."

Chapter Twelve

Bobbi liked Sin's parents, and she felt fairly sure they liked her. Sin was polite, even friendly, but he deliberately kept himself apart from them, and she found that difficult to understand.

"You have hostility down to a science," she said quietly as she and Sin sat side by side at the table in the inn's dining room while Sin's parents and Gina and Patrick danced on the dining room's tiny dance floor. "You have your father so off balance, he doesn't know what to say to you. But your mother's on to you."

He gave her a quick glance that showed her he was hurt and didn't like it. "I'm doing my best," he said. "They're here for you and the baby, anyway, not for me."

"You mean you're jealous."

"I mean I'm not going to pretend to be thrilled to see them when I'm not the reason they came."

"Would they have come to see me and the baby had I not been married to you and had this not been your baby?"

He gave her an impatient glance. "Don't try to psychoanalyze the situation, okay? I know it better than you do."

"I don't care about the situation," she replied. "It's you I'm worried about."

"Then you can stop. I'm fine."

They watched the dancers in silence. The music changed and so did the partners. Patrick led Janice across the floor in a seductive tango, while Douglas and Gina did a stepped-up waltz to it. Baldwin was smoking a cigarette on the terrace.

"I'll bet you never call *them,* either," Bobbi said, her chin rested on her hand as her toe beat time to the music. She smiled at Sin, though she didn't turn to look at him. "It's easier that way, isn't it? Just like you did with me. Wait for them to come to you. You're never rejected that way."

"Bobbi..."

"But they're getting older, you know. You put off forgiveness much longer and it could turn out to be too late."

He made a sound of impatience. "It's not a matter of forgiveness. It's a matter of... need. There was a time when they didn't need me. Now I don't need them."

"If you didn't need to hold on to them, why did you join your father's firm? Why didn't you go out on your own?"

He shrugged. "It was easier."

Bobbi shook her head and gave him an indulgent smile. "You never do the easy thing, Sin. That's why you have to do this. Your child will need grandparents, and I haven't any to give it."

He groaned at her persistence. "Why are you doing this?" he demanded.

"Because I love you," she replied without having to think about it, "and because love is a far more nurturing environment than resentment and old grudges."

Sin leaned back in his chair, weary of the argument. "Sweetheart, stay out of it," he said.

"I'm in it, sweetheart." She leaned back with him, hooking her arm behind him and resting her forearm on his shoulder. "I didn't want to be. I wanted to be solitary and safe and exclusive, but you dragged me into love and trust and commitment, and I like it here. I'm not letting go of you so you can slide back into an emotional pout."

Sin turned his head to look into her eyes, his filled with warning. "You're on dangerous ground, woman," he said.

She gave an unconcerned tilt of her eyebrow. "You taught me that anything else wasn't worth the stroll. Want to dance? We can change partners with your mother. You can invite them for Christmas."

"I don't..."

"Janice!" Bobbi said, giving Sin a warning look as his mother sat opposite them. She turned a bright smile on her. "We were just talking about how much fun it would be to have you and Douglas to the cabin for Christmas."

Janice looked from Bobbi to her son. She studied him carefully, and Bobbi saw Sin lower his eyes without saying a word. There was an instant's pain in Janice's expression, then she turned back to Bobbi with a smile.

"Thank you. That would have been lovely," she said. "But we're expected in Gstaad for the holidays. We'll be back in January, though, in time for the baby's arrival." She turned a bland smile on Sin. "Certainly you won't mind if we visit Bobbi and the baby in the hospital?"

Before he could reply, the rest of their party reappeared for another round of coffee, and conversation and laughter hummed and buzzed around the table. Bobbi saw Douglas sit beside Janice, note her hasty sip of water and leaned closer to say something.

Janice shook her head and smiled, then turned to listen to Patrick, who was relating a joke on Gina.

Bobbi spent a quiet moment with Janice a little later as they waited for the men to retrieve their coats. Gina had run to the ladies' room.

"I'm sorry about Sin's..." Bobbi began.

Janice put an arm around her and smiled. "Thank you for caring how I feel. Actually Sin's justified in being resentful. We were too busy to give him much of our time when he was a child. In our minds, we were building a business to hand over to him, and thought a steady schedule here at home was a better way for him to live than the merry-go-round we were on. But we *were* involved in our work and I guess we sacrificed him for it. By the time he was in high school, he was hostile when we tried to spend time together. In college, he preferred to go to Patrick's for breaks and holidays."

She smiled wryly and shook her head. "I think we thought the day would come when he became an adult when he would understand what we were trying to do and forgive us. I don't think things were quite as bad as he remembers, but when you're hurt, memory can be pretty selective." She paused, and Bobbi saw in her eyes that she wasn't quite as philosophical about the situation as she pretended to be. "So far, it hasn't happened. I hope we haven't forfeited our roles as parents and grandparents."

"I'll work on him," Bobbi promised.

Janice squeezed her shoulders. "You do that. Despite what he's probably told you, we love him very much. We just made some foolish choices."

The men returned and conversation stopped as coats were donned for the chilly walk up the hill to Patrick and Gina's where everyone, Baldwin included, was spending the night.

Bobbi sighed as she took Sin's arm, torn between wanting to give him a punch in the gut, and wanting to put her arms around him because the old anger apparently went a lot deeper than she'd realized.

RAIN DRUMMED against the windshield as Sin and Bobbi drove home. There'd been a sudden and complete change in the weather, and Bobbi swore the change went deeper than cold fronts and pressure systems. She felt it in Sin.

Buttercup was curled up in the back of the Blazer beside a plastic-wrapped antique high chair Gina and

Patrick had found for their baby and asked Bobbi to refinish.

"Want me to drive for a while?" Sin looked tired, she thought. She imagined holding on to grudges was hard work.

He gave her a quick glance that held the barest trace of amusement, then looked back to the road. He turned up the speed on the windshield wipers.

"Thanks anyway. You wouldn't fit behind the wheel."

Bobbi patted her protruding tummy. "She'll remember that you were mean to her mother, you know."

He glanced her way again. This time his smile actually formed. "She?"

"Yes. The baby's beginning to feel feminine. She's very quiet when I'm eating or watching the soaps. But she kicks me when we watch football."

He laughed softly. "Maybe she's just practicing to participate."

"I think she's registering her disapproval."

"Or she's a he."

She sighed and rested her head back. "That would be nice if Gina had a girl. Then our son could marry their daughter and no matter what happened, we'd all be friends forever because we'd have grandchildren in common."

Sin reached behind him for the blanket and tossed it over her one-handed, keeping a careful eye on the road.

For a moment there was just the sound of rain beating against the car and the whoosh of the tires on the wet road. Dusk fell like a dark, wet canopy.

"Sin?" she asked softly.

He knew what was coming. It had been on the tip of her tongue since he'd said a polite but cursory goodbye to his parents that afternoon. He didn't want to talk about it.

When he continued to stare at the road in silence, she went ahead without waiting for his response. "I'll bet they're not really expected in Gstaad."

"They've gone to Gstaad for Christmas before."

"Your mother knew you'd remember that and she thought you'd believe her."

"I do."

"I don't."

He let the silence tick a moment. "But she's not your mother, is she?"

"She's supposed to be. Because I'm married to her son, I become a part of her family—like another child. Particularly since my own mother's gone."

"Bobbi, please," he said patiently. "I married you to be your husband, not to help you replace your parents."

"I was thinking about our baby's grandparents."

"We are not inviting them to spend the holidays with us," he said clearly and succinctly. "End of discussion."

She slipped down into the blanket, feeling tired and depressed. "But it's not the end of your relationship. Someday you'll have to deal with it."

"Be quiet," he said, "and go to sleep."

December

IT RAINED ALMOST NONSTOP into the first week of December, then there were two crisp, cold sunny days where the temperature dropped into the teens.

Sin and Bobbi took long, slow walks up and down the road, Buttercup prancing along at the end of a leash.

Bobbi had refinished the cradle, and it now sat at the foot of their bed, the small quilt she'd bought at the bazaar laundered and resting in it, waiting for the baby.

Bobbi worked on the pieces from the bazaar, while Sin continued to cook and keep a careful eye on her progress. He spent his spare time poring over files that arrived by messenger from his office.

They never mentioned his parents.

The atmosphere between them was loving and warm but a natural tension was created by the seemingly irreconcilable difference of opinion. They resolutely worked around it, Sin determined that it would make no difference between them, Bobbi determined to change his mind about Christmas.

"Are presents out of the question?" Bobbi asked when sunshine streamed into the kitchen on the third bright but arctic-cold morning.

He was frowning over the front page of the *McMinnville News Register* and absently sipping coffee. She spread jam on her last triangle of toast.

"Presents for whom?" he asked without looking up.

"Your mom and dad," she replied intrepidly.

She watched him closely for a reaction. No one else would have noticed it, but she saw the dimple form under the corner of his mouth. That only happened when he clenched his jaw.

"I always send them a fruit basket through the office," he replied finally, still without looking up.

There was an instant's silence.

"Whee," she said flatly.

He put his cup down and looked up at her, temper alive in his eyes. But underlying it, she saw frustration, and knew it wasn't solely because of her. He'd been thinking about his parents since their visit to Candle Bay, she felt sure of it. But he didn't want to. She was sure of that, too.

"You just put *yourself* off the presents list," he said as he folded up the paper and put it aside. "Santa not only keeps lists of the naughty and the nice, but the nags as well."

She smiled and reached across the table for his hand. "That's what wives do. If you didn't want to subject yourself to that, you should have remained single. The brass on that old ship's lamp we got at the bazaar buffed up beautifully. And your mother told me the study in their London house has a nautical decor. I'll bet they'd like it."

Sin resented the suggestion, primarily because it seemed like a good idea and probably was the right thing to do. He also resented that she'd taken to his parents so quickly and so completely. Her innate warmth and enthusiasm made it hard for him to hold on to the old anger. But he intended to as long as he could.

"Fine," he said, going to the counter for the coffee carafe. "We'll box it up and ship it to London. They won't get it until they get home from Gstaad, but..."

"They're in L.A.," she said, holding her cup out for more coffee, looking up at him wide-eyed when he stopped in the act of pouring.

"How do you know that?" he asked quietly.

"Your secretary told me yesterday when she called with those figures you asked for for that breach of contract thing you're working on."

"And how did the subject of my parents come up, I wonder?"

She touched his hand to tip coffee into her cup, then she smiled smugly. "Apparently your parents told your secretary how much they like me, and how wonderfully you're taken to domestic bliss."

"Really."

"Yes. And she didn't know anything about Gstaad but she overheard them telling someone else at the office that they'll be staying in the States until after the baby's born and they're sure everything's all right."

"Fine." He got to his feet. "We'll send the lamp to Los Angeles. Let's do it this morning. According to the news, the weather's about to turn."

She smiled excitedly. "Snow?"

It took everything he had not to smile back. "By tonight. We'd better get our Christmas tree while we're at it."

She came around the table to wrap him in a hearty hug. He resisted holding her for all of three seconds, then enveloped her in his embrace, delighting in the way she snuggled in, as though sure she belonged there. Then he gave her a half-punitive, half-affectionate slap on her bottom and sent her to get her coat.

"IT ISN'T TALL ENOUGH," Bobbi insisted.

Sin inspected the Douglas fir he held at arm's length. It was half again as tall as he was. "It's over nine feet, Bobbi. How tall do you want it?"

"It's a two-story living room," she said, pointing to a fat fifteen-footer. "How about that one?"

He let the long-suffering Christmas tree lot clerk replace the tree he held and went to distract Bobbi from Paul Bunyan's tree. He spotted another that was about twelve feet. "What about this one? With a star or an angel on it, it'll scrape the ceiling."

The lot clerk pulled it out and Bobbi walked slowly around it. "You're sure it's tall enough?" she asked worriedly.

"I'm sure."

"It's a little thin back here."

"We'll turn that side to the wall."

She stepped back and tilted her head to the side like an artist mentally framing a prospective still life. "It is nice and straight, if a little short."

"We'll take it," he told the boy, who smiled in relief.

"You're sure you don't want the fifteen-foot one?" Bobbi asked, following Sin to the trailer to pay.

He grinned down at her as the boy made change. "Are you going to climb the ladder to decorate the upper branches? All we have is a six-foot ladder."

She kissed his jaw. "We could hang you by your toes from the gallery."

"Keep it up," he threatened. "You slipped off Santa's list this morning. Now you're falling off mine."

"You already bought my present," she said, standing beside him while he helped the boy ease the tree, bottom first, through the tailgate.

He finally gave her his frowning attention. "How do you know that?"

"I saw it. But I didn't look inside."

"I put it under the bed."

"I was trying to find my slipper."

He gave her a skeptical look as he helped her into the seat and closed her door.

"You couldn't have been snooping," he said, slipping in behind the wheel. He gave her a quick, dry glance as he pulled out onto the road. "Like you did when my office called yesterday?"

She gave a dramatic gasp. "I'm affronted by the suggestion." Then she smiled winningly. "Can we get a pizza? If you're going to put the tree up this afternoon I'm going to need my strength to supervise."

"You don't get off that easily. Someone has to decorate the bottom while I'm hanging off the gallery."

"Then I'll need pizza *and* cheesecake."

He turned in the direction of Shakey's. "Whatever. They're your hips."

There was a moment's silence, then she asked plaintively, "You think they're getting fat?"

He laughed and reached out to catch her hand. "No. I think all of you is getting perfect."

"Sin!" she said in a whisper, pointing through the windshield. "Look!"

Snow dusted down as if it were some beautiful invasion—slow, silent flakes of formidable size raining from a leaden sky. Everyone on the street stopped to look up.

Bobbi craned her head to do the same. "I saw snow once on a high-school trip to Big Bear, and once a few years ago when we had that freaky winter and there was snow for a couple of hours in L.A. Gina and I drove to the foothills to see it."

He squeezed the hand he still held. "Then we'll have to take a walk in it before we put the tree up."

Bobbi turned to him with a suggestive smile. "Gstaad has nothing on us today, has it?"

After lunch, Bobbi ran into the ladies' room, then remembered that she hadn't taken her Brethine. She pulled out a small collapsible cup she kept in her purse and downed the pill.

"Hi!"

Bobbi turned to find one of the clerks who'd helped her in the boutique when she'd first arrived in Felicity walk into the ladies' room.

"You're looking wonderful," the clerk said, even as she frowned at her own reflection. "Wait till you have this baby and it keeps you up all night. Then, you'll look like me. When are you due?"

"First week in January," Bobbi replied.

The young woman winked at her in the mirror. "Then get your rest now. Trust me."

Sin drove home slowly, the interior of the Blazer filled with the fragrance of Christmas. The outside world was also doing its best to generate atmosphere. Snow now fell heavily, and the roadside was already covered with white.

The chevron-shaped tops of the trees were snow-tipped, and fences and telephone poles began to collect caps of it.

Bobbi turned to Sin, reaching out to touch his arm. "I don't ever remember being this happy," she said gravely.

He gave her a quick glance, despite the slick road. It was filled with love and affection and gratitude. "Neither do I. Not even close."

Sin changed his mind about the walk the moment he helped Bobbi out of the Blazer. The snow was the wet, slippery variety rather than the dry, crunchy stuff, and he had to hold her firmly all the way to the door for fear she'd slip.

She had to content herself with sitting near the window with a cup of cocoa and watching the snow from the warmth and safety of the kitchen.

By evening the romantic tone of the storm had changed to one of fury. The wind howled and drove the snow sideways. Bobbi still enjoyed it. She guessed that watching it from the window was a little similar to living in the middle of a snow machine.

Sin had been moving busily around the cabin for the last hour or so, carrying wood in, and going in and out of the garage.

She looked up at him as he placed an oil lamp on the kitchen table.

"Very atmospheric," she said, "but wouldn't candles be moodier?"

"I think we're going to lose power pretty soon," he said, trimming the wick. "It's pretty predictable around here when the wind blows."

As though on cue, the lights flickered.

"That's why you filled the wood box."

"Right. We may end up having sandwiches for dinner."

She patted the baby complacently. "That's fine. We're full of pizza anyway."

He leaned over and kissed her. "And a major portion of baloney. Come and sit by the fire. This window's getting to be like an ice cube."

He did get soup heated before the power went. They shared it and a sandwich by the light of the oil lamp, and drank coffee he'd prepared ahead and put in a thermos.

"You're wasted as an attorney," Bobbi said, sipping the hot brew, enjoying the way the light burnished his hair.

"So I've been told by a few clients," he said.

She scolded him with a look. "I mean that you have such wonderful domestic talents. You should run an orphanage, or a halfway house for women weary of the world."

His eyebrow went up. "Married three weeks and you're trying to pawn me off on other women?"

"Only emotionally." She broke a butterflake roll in half and buttered it lightly, giving him a grinning glance. "The lovemaking you have to save for me. But I'll bet half the world's wives would pay big money to come to you and have their diets analyzed, their meals prepared, their every need seen to." She tore a small piece off the half and popped it into her mouth. "I could be your business manager," she went on. Then she frowned thoughtfully. "But that would keep you pretty busy and we want to make sure you still have time for me. I mean, what if we decided to do this again? We wouldn't want you all tied up with *other* pregnant women."

"True." He poured more coffee. "Why don't I just write a book telling other husbands how to do it?"

She leaned her chin on her hand and smiled at him. "I find it hard to believe there could be another man in the world with the degree of skill you have. Even with the help of a book."

Her eyes held complete sincerity. The temptation to snatch her up and make love to her was torturous. But she looked tired and a little pale, and the closer she came to term, the more he began to worry about her safety and that of the baby. The doctor had reassured both of them over and over that everything should be fine, but he knew the unforeseen always lurked, waiting to catch the unwary.

He decided to please her instead of himself.

"Just for that," he said, getting up to reach into the freezer that was no longer working, "you get a bonus."

She sat up greedily. "What?"

He took a plate from the cupboard and brought the freezer-wrapped package to the table. "Frozen penuche," he said. "It should be edible in an hour or so."

"You froze a batch?" she demanded in delight. "What made you think to do something so clever?"

"The knowledge that you'd have eaten both batches at one time, if I hadn't stashed the second one."

She smiled at him across the golden lamplight. "Do you suppose I could have a backrub while the fudge is thawing?"

"Sure." He helped her to her feet and carried the kitchen chair along as he walked her to the fire. "Let's see how the storm's doing." He turned on the portable radio.

He eased her into the kitchen chair, her side leaning against the back, and began to massage her. They listened to several country-Western tunes before the broadcaster's voice broke in with a news bulletin.

Power and telephone service would not be restored before morning because of the conditions, and visibility on the highway was virtually zero. The highway would be sanded overnight, but outlying roads were sheets of ice and everyone was advised to stay home.

"The phone service is out, too?" Bobbi asked.

"Guess so," Sin replied, his long fingers working gently but firmly along her weary spine. "Hey, relax.

You're stiffening up on me. I haven't had occasion to call anyone, so I hadn't noticed." He gave her hip a gentle rub that had nothing to do with massage.

"We'll just have to load on extra blankets tonight. We've got lots of groceries. If you go easy on the fudge, we should be cozy for four or five days anyway."

"That's . . . good," she said.

"We'll leave the drapes open, then I'll move the sofa bed in front of the fire and we'll watch the snow till we can't keep our eyes open."

She sighed and leaned trustingly back into his hands. "That'll be nice," she whispered.

HE FELL ASLEEP sometime after ten with Bobbi's and the baby's weight propped against him. He dozed off thinking he was going to have to cut her off the junk food and make her stick to the diet. She looked big-eyed and peaked tonight, and that made him nervous. If anything happened to her or the baby now, he didn't know what he'd do.

He awoke, startled and concerned, into almost complete darkness. It took him a moment to focus on what had awakened him. His arms were empty.

He sat up. "Bobbi?"

"Yes?" she replied instantly.

He turned his head to the sound of her voice and saw her shadowy form crouched in front of the fire. "What are you doing?" he asked, climbing out of the sofa bed. He felt anxious and edgy and tried to shake the mood off.

"Trying to rebuild the fire," she said. There was a note of self-deprecation in her voice, and something else—something that was seldom there. Fear.

He got down on his knees beside her and found that she'd pulled on her red coat over her nightgown.

"Go back to bed," he said. "I'll do it."

"No," she said quietly. "I need to pace. Want a cup of tea?"

The power of the fear now made her voice small, and he stopped working over the fire to turn and look at her. In the glimmer of flame that remained he saw in her eyes what was frightening her.

Fear caught *him* in its clutch and tried to pull him in. No. Not tonight. Not with the roads impassable, the power out and the phone lines down. No. It had to be something else. Please let it be something else. "Indigestion?" he asked, hoping against hope.

She gave him a frail little smile. "If I were Godzilla, this might be indigestion. For a woman of fairly normal size, I'd say it's labor."

Chapter Thirteen

"The pills stopped working?" he demanded in surprise.

She shook her head and lowered her eyes, pulling her coat more tightly around her. "I...think I forgot them in the ladies' room of the restaurant at lunch."

"What?"

"I know," she said defensively, "but I ran into one of the clerks from the boutique where we got my clothes, and we got to talking about babies and I..." She shook her head in frustration as though just how it had happened was a matter she'd worried over for some time. "I... think I just left them on the counter. I didn't think about them until after dinner when I went to take them ... and I didn't have them."

"Why in the hell ... ?" he began heatedly, fear for her making his usually rational reaction to crisis take a serious nosedive.

"Why did I do it?" she shouted at him. There was anger as well as fear in her eyes now. "Obviously because I wanted to upset you! Because I wanted to go into labor while stranded seven miles from town with no way to get to the hospital or bring help here! Because I've been looking forward to doing this all by myself while you—!''

Curiously her tirade restored his balance. He took hold of her shoulders and she stopped.

''The question was going to be,'' he said quietly, ''why didn't you tell me when you first realized you didn't have your pills?''

She subsided, shifting her weight, then wincing when it caused discomfort. ''Because the power and the phone were already out, and the guy on the radio said the roads were a mess. I had a backache by that time, but I didn't see any point in worrying you until I was sure. I thought it might go away.''

Sin continued to resist the inevitable. ''Dr. Fletcher said that some women taken off the medication in their ninth month sometimes are two weeks overdue.''

She shrugged and made a helpless gesture with her hands. ''I'm not going to be one of them, Sin. I think I'm just going into the second phase. Help me up, please. I need to walk around.''

Sin stood and, bracing her forearms, helped her to her feet. She leaned her full weight on him, and that reminded him that she needed him, that all his talk about being a part of her life and the baby's was all lip service if he wasn't willing to lend his hand to *this* part.

''I'll try the phone again,'' he said.

''I already did. It's still out.''

He turned to the window they'd left undraped for the night and saw snow whirling past it as the wind continued to howl. Trying to drive to town could be more dangerous than staying home and hoping phone service would be restored before she delivered.

"When you brought me here," she said softly, still holding his forearms, "you said we were going to make this baby together. I have a feeling we're literally going to do that." She laughed thinly, a sob catching in her throat. "Still got your book? Ah!"

She went rigid under his hands. Supporting her weight, he found himself counting. It was almost sixty seconds before she relaxed and drew several deep breaths. If the book could be trusted, and it certainly could so far, a longer contraction definitely indicated second-phase labor.

She started to walk and he stayed with her. "We're finally going to see what she looks like," Bobbi said.

"And whether or not she's wearing a Gold's Gym T-shirt."

He hugged her and rubbed her back. "Everything's going to be fine. Dr. Fletcher and my trusty book say thirty-three-week babies are usually safe. That's just about what we've got here."

Lung development was sometimes a problem, but he decided to keep that to himself. He also remembered the doctor saying the use of medication to stop preterm labor often stressed the baby's lungs to develop more quickly. If God was in His heaven, the Gold's Gym baby was going to come out screaming.

"I'm going to put you down on the bed for a few minutes," he said, lifting her to carry her there. "I'll rebuild the fire, chip some ice for you to suck on if there's any left and get a few other things we'll need. Don't move, okay? Promise?''

"Promise."

He was horrified to discover his hands were shaking. He rebuilt the fire, then disappeared into the kitchen to pour himself a brandy and down it in one swallow before he did anything else.

In a moment the warmth blazed a path down his chest and settled comfortably in his stomach. The liquor and his innate possessiveness helped him regain control and focus his energy.

His woman was having *his* baby. And he was going to deliver it. Nothing happened to what was his. He wouldn't let it.

She was breathing heavily when he came back with a bowl of ice chips. He couldn't have made a mixed drink with what was left in the freezer, but for their purposes, the little shards that remained were perfect.

"Another contraction?" he asked, banking the pillows behind her head.

She nodded. "Okay. Tell me when the next one starts. Here." He spooned ice into her mouth.

She closed her eyes and made a sound of approval.

"We never decided," she said after a moment, "between Janeil and Ariel."

"Or Travis and Nicholas. Why are you so sure it's a girl?" He pulled her gently onto her side and rubbed the base of her back. "You don't think we have one of each, do you?"

"Right now it feels like a whole drill team," she said. "Oh, Sin. That feels so good. Maybe it'll calm her down, too. I think she's primping for her big entrance.''

''A boy could just be clearing the decks, making his space.''

He moved his hand to the front of her to massage her stomach. He felt her stiffen slightly.

''Another one,'' she said.

He looked at his watch: 3:17. Then he felt the bulbous shape under his hand turn to solid rock. Bobbi pushed back into the pillow, eyes closed, jaw set. The moment seemed interminable. Then the peak of the contraction was over and she began to relax, drawing deep, ragged breaths.

''Can you get me another pillow?'' she asked, her voice husky. ''These aren't quite supporting me.''

''I've got a better idea.''

Sin climbed onto the bed behind her and pulled her back against him, holding her to him just above the mound of her stomach.

''The book says this should be comfortable for you,'' he said.

''Ha!'' she scoffed with more good humor than derision.

He laughed. ''Well, I'm sure comfort is a relative term in this situation. Hold onto your knees. That's it. Okay, tell me when it starts.''

Her contractions were roughly five minutes apart for the next two hours. He bathed her face, spooned ice into her mouth and read the chapter on delivery while she leaned against him. It scared the hell out of him.

Then there was a sudden and alarming change. He felt her legs, splayed against his, ripple with the pain of the contraction, and for the first time, she cried out.

He felt it with her.

Then she sagged against him and said with weak humor, "This is not fun, Sinclair. We're adopting the next one."

"Whatever you say," he promised. At that moment he'd have promised her a platonic relationship for the rest of their married lives. "How you doing? The ice is down to water. Want some?"

"Please."

He reached around her to offer her the spoon. Then dipped the washcloth he'd also brought in and wiped her face with it.

"Jeez," she whispered harshly. "Here it comes again!"

He checked his watch. Two minutes apart.

He held her as she went rigid. She pressed into him for support and he offered everything he had, the sturdiness of his frame surrounding her, the comfort and encouragement of every tender word he knew, the stroke of his hands as the pain subsided and she collapsed against him, panting.

"The good part about this phase," he said, mopping her brow, "is that it only lasts about fifteen minutes."

"Yeah," she said wryly, "and then I get to deliver. Is it too late to go back to phase one? That wasn't so bad. I even . . . Oh, God!"

As soon as the contraction was over, he slipped out from behind her and helped her sit up.

"Where are you going?" she asked nervously.

"Nowhere. I have to get a few things ready here. You seem to be progressing very efficiently according to the book. You don't want Janeil to come out into the world with no one to catch her."

He dampened the cloth again and bathed her face. She smiled weakly at him.

"Do you still have my heart earrings?" she asked.

It took him a moment to switch gears from imminent childbirth to a discussion of jewelry. He bathed her face again, wondering if she was getting delirious on him.

"Ah...yeah. In the rolltop box on the dresser."

"Good." She smiled. "My father gave those to me when I turned sixteen."

He'd never thought much about her parents, but he wondered now, at this curious time, about the man and woman who'd probably been together much like this twenty-six years ago. Knowing her now as he did, loving her, he felt a sense of loss that he'd never met the people who'd created her.

"They're beautiful earrings," he said. "I noticed them the afternoon of the wedding."

"You know why hearts are shaped the way they are?" she asked, making a heart shape with her hands by holding her thumbs together in a point and dipping her forefingers together.

Then she clenched them into fists as another contraction overtook her. She grabbed for him and he put an arm around her to support her. He felt sweat break out on his forehead as she screamed.

Then she panted her relief and he put her back against the pillows. He pulled the sheet over her, folded the foot back and slipped towels under her.

"You know why?" she asked.

For a moment, he didn't remember the question. Then it came back to him. Hearts.

"Why are they shaped the way they are?"

She made the shape with her fingers again, and wiggled her thumbs that made the point at the bottom. "My father said it's because the heart was made to hold things in the bottom of it," she said. "Things we think have spilled out, or been lost, are caught in the bottom of our hearts. Like you were."

He looked up from his preparations to catch her pain-filled, love-filled eyes. "I didn't want you to be the right man because I was afraid of your life-style, afraid of you. For four months I tried to put you out of my mind. In Candle Bay on Memorial Day weekend, I wanted you to know I wanted no part of you."

He kissed her knee before going to the pot of water he had placed on the grate in the fireplace. "The message was pretty clear," he said.

"But the moment I saw you at Rebecca's," she went on, "I remembered the night you made love to me. Every little detail came back to me because I'd never really lost it. It was all there, in the bottom of my heart."

He washed his hands and he washed her, thinking how much he'd changed from the man who'd made love to her that night.

She'd been in the bottom of his heart all right, he thought. Rooted there, filling his heart, overflowing it, brimming in his mind and his senses so that everything within him was her. And that was how he felt at this moment. And the responsibility for her safety and that of their baby made him weak with terror.

But he didn't let himself think about it. He had to get a basin, pull her to the end of the bed, prop her feet on kitchen chairs.

"Oh, God, Sin," she said, her voice raspy with weariness and excitement and fear. "I feel her! She's coming."

CLUTCHED IN A GIANT FIST of pain, Bobbi felt her confidence waver. Who were they to think they could safely deliver their child four weeks early without a medical person in attendance? Surely it would be safer to wait for someone to arrive, or for the roads to clear so that they could drive to town.

Then she felt the baby bang against her, as though giving one giant rap on the door to the world. It reverberated through Bobbi's entire lower body.

"I see her head, Bobbi," Sin shouted. "Push!"

It occurred to her to laugh at herself for even considering that the baby would wait until conditions improved. If it were anything like her, it wouldn't listen, and if it were anything like its father, it would do whatever it damn well pleased.

But laughter was a far cry from what she felt like doing at that moment. The worry was as excruciating as the pain, and all she could do was concentrate on the job at hand and give it all she had.

Pain squeezed her, pounded on her, and grew even stronger. She held her breath and pushed, wanting nothing more in this world than to expel this child from her body and into its father's hands.

"Almost!" Sin shouted at her. She felt his hand rub her knee and down her thigh. "Come on, Bobbi. This time Janeil is coming out."

Without giving her an instant to rest the pain crested again, covered her world and choked it. But for all her insistent hammering on the door, Janeil waited on the other side.

Bobbi sagged back after the contraction, but its absence gave no relief. She felt as though she would burst at any moment.

Pain rumbled over her again. She grunted and pushed.

"No, don't tense up!" Sin called to her. "Just push!"

She wanted to ask him if he wanted to do this, but she couldn't push and speak at the same time. Then she felt the barest, fractional relief and Sin shouted.

"Here she comes! We've got a head, Bobbi!"

Then there was no stopping her. She concentrated and pushed without tensing. She prayed and pushed and prayed and pushed.

"Right shoulder. Left sh—whoa!" A satisfied laugh followed Sin's surprised exclamation.

Then there was silence. A long, interminable, complete silence. Sin held the slimy little red bundle in his hands and felt a moment's panic when it simply lay there. Then he remembered what he was supposed to do—stroke the sides of the nose downward, the neck and under the chin upward.

Bobbi, laying back in exhausted relief, heard the silence and felt fear rush up through her like a ramming fist.

She pushed herself up on her elbows just in time to hear a hesitant cry, followed by a screech of disapproval and indignation.

"Is she all right?" she demanded of Sin, who was tucking the baby into a towel.

For an instant, Sin couldn't even share the baby with Bobbi. This was his. He'd planted it, he'd nurtured it, and he'd brought it into the world. He stared at it in amazement. His. God. He felt humbled and exalted all at once.

"The baby's fine," he said, placing it on Bobbi's stomach. "But, he's Travis and not Janeil." He wrapped his arms around her and pulled her up to the pillows. Then he stopped, looked deeply into her eyes and kissed her soundly. "Well done, my love." He grinned. "And no Gold's Gym T-shirt."

"It's a boy?" she asked in amazement. "I was so sure."

"I kept telling you you were mistaking grand jetées for place kicks."

Bobbi looked at the baby, red and wrinkled and squalling, and thought he was probably the most beautiful child ever born of woman. A true miracle. And considering how things had worked out between her and Sin, it was indeed a miracle.

"I can't believe we did it," she said, smiling up at Sin in wonder. "We have a son."

He sat beside her, his arm around both of them. Love rushed through him. It filled every little corner of his being. He felt it change everything he'd known. This little being was part of him, and part of Bobbi, their love for each other personified.

"I love you so much," he said, his voice thick with emotion, "the words seem shallow and meaningless. What I feel is so strong there probably isn't a word for it. I don't know how I can make you understand what it is."

She pulled his head down to rub her cheek against his. "I share it with you, Sin. I feel it, too. It's so big that description can't contain it." She kissed him, then leaned wearily against him. "Do you realize that you delivered our baby?" She laughed weakly, her voice high and strained. "Now your business cards can say, Paul Sinclair, attorney and midwife."

He laughed softly at the notion. "You just lay there and rest. I've got a little more work to do here, then I'm going to try the phone again. And have a drink!"

"WANT TO HIRE ON?" Dr. Fletcher asked him with a broad grin in the emergency room. "You did good work. Your patients are in fine health."

"Thanks," Sin said, feeling the energy begin to drain out of him, the sapped adrenaline leaving exhaustion in its place. "I don't think my nerves could take it."

"I'm keeping the three of you until tomorrow morning," the doctor said, frowning into his face. "I'm putting you in the birthing room so you can be together. I think you all need some rest."

"You're sure the baby's all right?"

"Perfect. Even a pretty good size. Six pounds, three ounces."

"And Bobbi?"

"Also perfect. If you feel up to it tonight, I'll even order you a bottle of champagne. But for now—I want you all to get some sleep."

SIN AWOKE to a lullaby sung in an off-key soprano. He pushed himself to a sitting position, thinking he'd never heard anything so beautiful in his life.

It had to be midnight or later, and Bobbi sat in a chair by the window that looked out onto the quiet black night, and nursed the baby.

His feelings were so strong he felt as though his body effervesced. Love for her, and love for Travis swelled up in him like champagne overflowing its glass. He went to stand behind the chair and leaned down to wrap both his arms around them.

"I'm sorry we woke you," she whispered. The baby suckled greedily, puffy eyes closed, tiny fingers fluttering. She leaned her head back into him.

"I was thinking," she said. Her voice sounded high and heavy. He squatted down beside the chair to look into her eyes, his own concerned. But she was smiling. "Eight months ago I was so sure making love with you had been a mistake." She uttered a funny little laugh that had a sob attached. "And now look at what I have. You..." she said, shaking her head as she looked down at him as though her good fortune mystified her. Then she looked at the baby and a tear spilled over. "And Travis. God."

He brushed her hair back and kissed away the tear. "I'm the lucky one. I want to climb onto the roof and tell the whole world what a beautiful son we have."

Bobbi smiled at him, a bright look in her eyes telling him whom she knew would love to hear the news. Then she lowered her eyes and tried to change the subject. She started talking about a middle name for Travis, but Sin didn't hear her.

He felt it happen. Things bubbled up from the bottom of his heart. Things he'd thought he'd forgotten. Things he'd thought no longer mattered. Times his mother had held him or his father had touched him. The rare family outings, the even rarer evenings together at home.

He wondered why they came to him so clearly. He'd seldom thought about them before, even forgotten they'd existed. The times he'd been left behind while his parents flew off to negotiate one deal or another had always come into sharper focus.

But he couldn't call them up at the moment. All he could remember was how much he'd treasured those family times and wanted things to be different. And now he had the opportunity to change them—if he wanted to.

He wondered momentarily if he were simply caught up in the emotion of the moment, then decided it didn't matter. The emotion of the moment was love and that was how he planned to live the rest of his life.

"You feel up to talking on the phone?" he asked Bobbi.

She looked at him in surprise. "Sure. But will there be anyone at your office at this hour?"

He shook his head. "Oh, probably some die-hard law clerk. But I was going to call my parents."

Her already bright eyes brightened further. "You were?"

"I thought I'd invite them for Christmas."

She cradled the baby in one arm and hooked the other around his neck. He tucked his beside hers under Travis and felt the baby's warmth and feather-weight.

She smiled in delighted amazement. This was such a big step for Sin. It also meant that their love had made him forgive his parents and bury past hurt and disappointment. And that would be such a benefit for the little life she held in her arms. "You mean it?" she asked.

He smiled at her, feeling as though he held all the world's treasures in his arms. "From the bottom of my heart."

Following the success of WITH THIS RING and
TO HAVE AND TO HOLD, Harlequin brings you

JUST MARRIED

SANDRA CANFIELD
MURIEL JENSEN
ELISE TITLE
REBECCA WINTERS

just in time for the 1993 wedding season!

Written by four of Harlequin's most popular authors, this
four-story collection celebrates the joy, excitement and
adjustment that comes with being "just married."

You won't want to miss this spring tradition, whether
you're just married or not!

AVAILABLE IN APRIL WHEREVER HARLEQUIN
BOOKS ARE SOLD

HARLEQUIN SUPERROMANCE®

HARLEQUIN SUPERROMANCE NOVELS WANTS TO INTRODUCE YOU TO A DARING NEW CONCEPT IN ROMANCE...

WOMEN WHO DARE!
Bright, bold, beautiful...
Brave and caring, strong and passionate...
They're unique women who know their
own minds and will dare anything...
for love!

One title per month in 1993, written by popular Superromance authors, will highlight our special heroines as they face unusual, challenging and sometimes dangerous situations.

Discover why our hero is camera-shy next month with:
#545 SNAP JUDGEMENT by Sandra Canfield
Available in April wherever Harlequin Superromance novels are sold.

HARLEQUIN®

AMERICAN ✦ ROMANCE®

Legendary lovers come to life once more in Judith
Arnold's newest Harlequin American Romance title...

*Just Like Romeo
and Juliet*

Touching the statue of Juliet in Verona, Italy, was supposed
to bring luck in love. But Gillian Chappell didn't feel very
lucky when the sexy stranger whose kisses set her soul on
fire turned out to be her father's most hated adversary.

Enemies and lovers... Could even Juliet save this star-
crossed pair?

Relive all the romance and the passion that made Romeo
and Juliet the ultimate love story. Don't miss Judith Arnold's
#482 JUST LIKE ROMEO AND JULIET, coming to you next
month.

ROMEO